waste heat

violet reason

Main Boiler, Aprilci Bulgaria, 1928

waste
heat

violet reason

calliope press sarasota 2008

acknowledgments
the following poems have been published before:
transtemporal telephoning, in the *Idahonian;* the stone, *The Argonaut*
not a passenger, *Blue Hen Review;* arson, in *Palouse*
autophagy, in *FourMile Review;* nuclear ambush, *San Fernando Poetry*
Review; the bakery thrift store, *San Fernando Poetry Review*
saturday night, *Leftovers;* in harry's used bookstore, *Tucson Book Review*
Several of these works have been published on internet sites;
several have been published in earlier versions in earlier books.
Works in the "senseless" section were assembled
from Violet Reason's notes by Yulalona Lopez.

Make-up art by Merissa dePasse & A.M. Caratheodory
Graphics by Ryan Garcia Calusa, Moscow, Idaho
redesign@riangarciacalusa.com

Publisher's Cataloging-in-Publication data
Violet Reason, 1945-2004
cheap visions/Violet Reason
I. Title.
PS3553.A644A898 2008

ISBN 978-0-911385-42-7 (paper)
Manufactured in the United States of America

3 Muses Books / Calliope Press
Sarasota, Florida /
editor@3musesbooks.com

Mozart and Reason Wolfe, ltd.
Wilmington, Delaware
mozart@reasonwolf.com

approximate contents

coyote redevivus

coyote cosmogenesis / coyote invents television
coyote steals a car / meets godzilla
coyote goes nuclear / takes a mate / gets analyzed
coyote steals ice cream / runs for mayor
coyote deconstructs / changes clothes / overextends

senseless

carbon dreams / machine dreams
school trap / ambiguous announcements
academic poultry / bags of water
gotta get to hell on time
mathematics of home equations
roll me / bonfire of creation
paion / faust reconsiders
still life with clothes
swimming at night
secret of life

homeless

stages of defeat / life goes on
mean of life / f-art
xxx-mas / ravenna freedom
alley angels / origins
tao of home / use of children
roll me again / the herd heads south
the herd rests / death in a teacup / three shadows

lifeless

every story ends in death
seeking good death
death writes clear obits / death practices by phone
death picks up / death talks to himself
death takes a vacation / death back at work
deadlines / picnic at swan point
death the final diet / death has a crisis
death practices joking / death gets personal
death meets his match

Dedications

Dedicated with deep respect to the memory of Violet Reason
        (1945-2004)
After receiving her MD from Columbia University, Dr. Reason
practiced medicine in Boston, an early pioneer of euthanasia
and self-mediated death (in 1975 she adopted this pen name
of Reason to protect her relatives and her colleagues, and a
second pen name, Babe Martin, to give voice to a homeless
friend). Not surprisingly, her beliefs and dedication cost her
her professional position, and she spent the rest of her life
exploring territories where doctors have rarely ventured. She
eventually made it to Florida, where she died homeless, but
not friendless, in July 2004.

And, dedicated fondly to the memory of Merissa DePasse
        (1945-1997)
After graduating in English from the University of Idaho, she
pursued a career in art, eventually designing books for Little
Brown in Boston, from *Ansel Adams* to *Mad* magazine. The
make-up painting in the colophon (as well as other books,
including *Carbon Dreams*, *Wild Apples* and *Two Diaries*)
were produced by her, working with her partner, A.M.
Caratheodory, over a productive and joyful 25 years. She was
working on her fourth novel, when she was killed in a cross
walk on Beacon Street by a drunk-driving nurse.

different perspectives

"is daikoku to be found here?" i asked.
"baatenda ni kite kudasai kare was nandemo shite imasu,"
 replied a patron of the nisi bar.

"Kono niku wa henna nioi shite imasu." Minori said.
"What? No way!" Erina answered.

"less is more" Robert Browning
"more or less" Oscar Wilde
"less is less" babe martin

cheap visions

a record of a life lived through the dreams of
others and by the means of luxury afforded
in a modern unbalanced industrial society

obvious truths

creation is the popcorn of existence
stars are fire
the earth is dirt
nature is different
god is indifferent
women are mean
men are cowards animals bite plants poison
life is short suffering is long
mathematics is uncertain nothing is as expected

misbegotten prophecies of geo. b. halstead (1819-1880)

trying to communicate distances over a hundred yards
is like shouting in the wind

man will never fly; he has no wings

the bottom of the ocean is as beyond our reach
as the moon

no one will ever travel as fast as a rabbit
much less a cheetah

we have enough coal for eternity and no need for anything else

people are the most valuable resource
machines will never replace men

science will be complete in a few years
and we will have a heaven on earth

in modest poverty

we are pavement dwellers
with no shelter   we are legless
crippled, dying   we have dragged
our scabby bodies over rock and mud
to see you   hear your offer

filth we are that but
we have no complaint knowing
nothing else   the sidewalk is our room
gutter our toilet   heaps of rags a bed
but services are free   sun is heating
rain and river plumbing   we live

where else could we go? we are
resigned to this the wheel will turn.
what will we ask of you who offer
everything beyond our dreams?
                five more feet of ground.

ddt dead cannibals

ddt dead cannibals lie at his feet—
they were the ones,
the top of the pyramid
who made a meal of people who ate the eggs
of birds that caught insects
that fed on plants sprayed
by people who felt that insects spoiled
the plants that were for animals
to eat so they could be eaten by people—
but now they're sorry they used ddt.

nuclear ambush
around the comer are intemperate natives
swaggering with megaton weapons
and distended bellies—we shouldn't be here but,
my, isn't it exciting?   just hold onto your purse,
i think that we can bluff our way past them,
with our doomsday attitude.

fear them? hell, we made them what they are
we can unmake them just as fast.
if they threaten us with violence
we'll cut off their wheat and condoms.
it was our selfless generosity that gave them
toilet paper and clean, white rice
it was christian sacrifice that sold
them longer lives and nuclear power
for television reruns—if they're not nice—

well, let 'em try it; they'll die trying;
they just can't take it like we can
just walk faster, straight ahead,
remember we have bigger bombs back home.

autophagy
the past is a source of anecdotes for us at parties.

we mine our thrown-away moments for ideas
in an archaeology of accidents.

we feed on long extinct experiences
like rotting meat from frozen mammoths,
then search our excrement for missing clues.

we smile and continue
to lick our fingers.

self love and human mythology

bigger is better, more is best, ah, not less,
ambition for size alone is the test,
the earth is infinite and
wealth is limitless

the more the merrier,
can't have enough children,
why we increase the chances
of an einstein or mozart with every
birth, and if they're poor,
why, they'll have all the more ambition.

but, for me to gain you must lose—
to get it back you must take it against my will.
choose and prepare to lose again.
hey, competition honed our skills
we're tops, apex of the pyramid,
omega point,
end of creation, strong, triumphant,
solid, and special—
we speak through the mask of superior
separateness
the quest for permanence, the lure
of the sleep of gold, perfect and permanent,
but cold in perfection,
the quest for something more, for honor,
duty, country, glory, and what's right this morning—
and if we're wrong, hell,
science will bail us out.

the bakery thrift store

women hopping in lines to
adrenaline sounds from speakers;
children fidgeting in the aisles over
hundreds of reduced-by-a-penny cupcakes.

see written in lines the desperation
of three-day-old stale bread, the urgency
of twenty loaves of roughage is confirmed
in brimming carts, the economy of bloated
housewives is evident in bargains offered
to speedy cashiers.

inscribed in foam the greed of consumers
who worship size and quantity—let them be
satisfied. let them rest sated on their sofas
and remember their last meal over
the suppressed groan of cells without
nourishment, humming to advertisements
of bigger savings.
                    from cellophaned manna
the world shall die with a bang
shot from cannons like puffed oats
and the meek shall inherit the crumbs.

life reconsidered as a function of sweet foods

1956-58	birthday cakes, halloween candy
1959	halloween candy, cookies
1960-62	orange slices
1963	powdered-sugar donuts
1964	chocolate milkshakes
1965	milkshakes still
1966	boston cream pies
1967	italian rum cakes, cream-filled donuts
1968	chocolate donuts, fruit sodas
1969	fudge, chocolate cupcakes
1970	chocolate/peppermint milkshakes
1971	plain cake donuts
1972	french pastries, sugar donuts
1973-74	brownies with ice cream
1975-76	chocolate-chip cookies
1977	iced angel food cakes
1978	swiss pastries, petit-fours
1979	pineapple sweet and sour prawns
1980	granola, with honey
1981	chocolate-chip cookies
1982-83	diet cookies, salt-free, sugar-free pretzels
1984-86	apples & dates
1987	chocolate-chip cookies
1988	chocodiles, mint cookies
1989	jelly rolls, ice cream
1990	chocolate-chip cookies
1991	sugared peanuts
1992	chocolate strawberries, peanut butter bars
1993	cream-filled donuts, brownies
1994	strawberry milkshakes, cookies
1995	dates, orange brownies, chocolate strawberries
1996	maple syrup, dates
1997	chocolate chip cookies
1998	chocolate marshmallow ice cream
1999	cream-filled chocolate-covered donuts

everyday heroes

harold grimaced in pain—
his nine-million-dollar foot hurt as
he limped onto the playing field.

shiela hugged the microphone to her breast
spotlighted on the stage moaning over
her recent drug addiction.

dick got off work at the chemical plant; after
a beer, he counted the money saved
for a brand new off-road motorcycle.

after half a cooling tv dinner, bill went back
to work on his book that outlined his plan
for world peace. the trailer was drafty so he got his sweater.

maureen finished putting china into the dishwasher;
she sat by her son, malcolm, and adjusted the wires and tubes.
malcom smiled and smiled.

american hate

ed has a chevy van, but i deserve it more
helen has a wrinkle-free complexion but she's a slut
johnny is so well-behaved (he's a dull little prick)

it's difference and unearned pleasure, diligence, luck,
and intelligence but most of all a determination
to be better than me—
can you believe it? aloofness and privacy,
or its lack, someone chummier than us, happiness
in any form, but especially without gain,
the ownership of goods, power in others hands, animals,
especially those who steal our profits by
eating seeds or clawing trees, untouched land—
there seems to be no explanation other
than hate, pure, simple, satisfying hate.

down congress street

"gotta have a dime buddy buy myself a hamburger—"
                "help the rescue mission
                        help the rescue mission!"

"anything you could spare sir for a loaf of bread?"

"flowers! flowers flowers! flowers for the handicapped!"

"spare change... any extra change? spare change?"

"the lord still lives-read about it! the lord still lives! read all
about it here! guru maharungi ji is the light; his is the way to save
mankind—buy now, special sale, only now."

one sits expectantly, quietly, asking for nothing

                "could you do me a favor, mister..."
"could i interest you in some clothes-wait! wait, look, i'll sell you
the whole bag for five dollars; no? four, how bout four—tell you
the truth mister, i could use a drink."

                shoe sale—40% off—brand names
        "do ya have a quarter i could borrow?"
    "gotta have a dime buy myself—" "help the—"
            "anything—" "look at these flowers! you—"
                "take one!" "thank the lord!" "could you—"
                "sorry..." "buddy, i just got off a train"
        i just kept walking there is a park on speedway
        sand where i can rest my head.

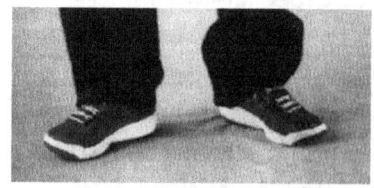

in harry's used bookstore

my favorites are the ones i looked at
in my youth: sweetly posed, airbrushed
into place. i feel better masturbating
to a familiar face, henchhh!

there's something unbecoming about
too much body hair; there's something
sterile about meat laid out with frozen smiles—
better to imagine what's hidden.

i collect all the old editions
and sometimes cut out poses of
my favorite naked ladies; keep
all them together in a folder.

i used to practice law, but i've gotten older
and i—oh, i still read a lot
about the random road to justice
and the current indecisions.

not one famous friend but if i did—
no, no, society's celebrity is worthless
under the shade of an orange tree.
i have a bottle in my pocket—try a swat.

mostly i just talk and look
around comforted by friends
on familiar ground— tell me what
you know about the age of clouds?

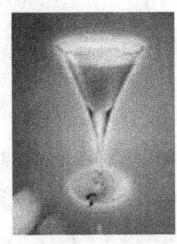

saturday night / academic men in love

       oh, baby, baby, i love your big 'b's!
your lobes they comfort me
in matters of philosophy.
no, no, i do not joke.
post hoc ergo propter hoc
is not a threat to those who know
the forms of logical fallacy.
       yes, more than merely 'a's or 'c's
i just love your big 'b's,
plump and grey and wrinkled—
their expanded surface area
makes our life together
an intellectual circus
and we both swing as from a trapeze
on constructs of words
and images with ease.
baby, baby, baby, baby,
       i love your big brains!
b, b, b, b, b! unh, unh, unhuh, unhuh ...

childless blues

here is what it means: no replacement,
no joe junior,
no cute girlie named after your favorite
aunt—oh, boo, hoo,
no blue booties, no young beauties,
and now it's too late too.
no, it's no disgrace, we waited 'til everything was right
but it never was and we are not and now it's too late too;
the sperms are warped and few, the womb untrue.
time passed, we delayed, we can't say we didn't choose
so we lie in the bed we made. no branches, no shoots
just the timely sweet decay as bodies fail to hold
together without good glue. still, there is a seed left
and who can deny that ideas are as faithful as genes.

the game of cowboys and maidens
she laughed for no reason,
no reason but a memory,
a memory of an almost forgotten episode,
forgotten episode of playing a game,
a game of lovers parting.

she with fluttering lashes over wide eyes
while the wind caressed her gingham dress
about the whitest, aching thighs;
he with a cowboy's laconic glance
toward the shrub in front of the cabin
and a muttered, unfulfilled good-bye.

it was only a lovers game,
a game of acting to pass time,
pass time to learn to prepare,
to prepare reasons for leaving,
for leaving time to laugh.

shock treatment
i will build another universe
somewhere we both can be.
all my universes are the same
they all have someone like you
and me, travelers in a dream,
until they're shaken from outside—
needles jump at the scream
silver lines rise on the graph
blue veins of electricity
lightning shatters the trace
into a multiplicity of bolts—
i see your face emerge
from a pregnant cloud—
how can you be sad
knowing what i am?

counting

i lay in bed on old stains of passion.
the world had stopped, events
everywhere tensed, massed

how long did we love, how many times,
was each happiness more than before,
was it simply a matter of addition,
and we who measure our lives by numbers
must have a way to remember the past:
count our money, list our deeds,
accumulate some photographs to display
our lives—except the lives
were only preparations for the films,
diplomas, memories, to be looked back on,
finished, accomplished, separated, framed
and hung on the living room wall?

how else can i evaluate the importance
of our lives? athletics, rooms, and trophies,
dances, dinners, and poses, how does it look?
struggles, reports, and stories, failure
and comic-book love, how does it read?
first a car, then a place, one love, then
six more—were any real?

reptile manners

if we fight, if we're angry, if you cross
me, i'll ruin you, cut you, crush you, abuse you—
        because i'm ugly, because the reptile
brain gains control of speech, because i need you
to be lower, because i need to destroy
you to rebuild you in the reptile image i want,
because it's power and it cannot go unused.

perhaps your rape would be rather thrilling
or perhaps a clever intellectual killing—
if you would be willing.

these two thumbs could make you blind
or use a board to break your spine—
if you wouldn't mind ...

if you're not unhappy, i'll haunt you, jump
down neural passageways thrust purifying light
and make your eyes observe the change
as you watch me rearrange your senses
and know the agony will grow.
i'll squeeze your heart if you stay apart
and weld a chain of inexpressible pain
to sanctify your being. enjoy darkness,
make peace with shadows or i'll burn them all away,
you can't hide from me, i distill from the water
you drink and every breath of air carries
me deeper in. i'll nestle in your spine
and move in your limbs
and flow on to your mind, your reptile mind,
the one that matches mine, and takes control,
i'll have your soul, as you took mine
(the power of words cannot go unused).

the social worker's guide to suicide
hey, suicide's not funny! it's not for fools.
you must follow certain rules:
first of all, wait for the moment
you can afford to be patient
death can overhaul you
and you want to go out right. next,
be sure you have the best of reasons;
depression isn't good enough—love! failure!
protest! these are what it's about.
then, don't ever do anything at night
unless you have dramatic lighting;
don't do anything at home
and don't do anything alone—an audience
is a must to observe the leap—no one

likes just finding the garbage. put yourself
in their place! don't do anything impulsive;
work toward the ideal situation.
once you've made the basic decision
for your destruction, think!
there's always a cliff that's higher,
another river deeper, faster, bluer,
another sharper wire, bullet truer.
if you feel a terrible need and can't resist,
relax! a little starvation or secret mutilation
will dissipate the tension, but leave you whole
for the final ending. take your time, it's
a one-way line, no second act or encore.

suicide rag

this is not a suicide note, just the progression of the thought,
the evolution of the goal—a goal not to be reached
before the accident or the sea.

1992: i see all of you gathered around the coffin, not
understanding why i have to leave in this way—that I could
not stand the pain, but grieving for yourselves. I wanted
to see your pain over mine one last time so i stopped
my heart with a bullet and that stopped all for me.
but you will go on and remember until you too have gone
on and no one remembers, even those who may read
these words, which will be nothing but a tattered shell
that echoes nothing. but, then, sophie goes before me,
and I see others grief first hand,
so I will wait another year.

1993: i write about suicide alone, into the sea.
but, frank goes before me, and the grief is too close.
and I cannot go.

1994: the time is right, circumstances have decreed,
the ties that bind have come unbound, but there is not enough
of a reason; the failed love, the lost job, the repossessed home

were not enough ... it would be too sudden, too much
like a single candle put out and not the end of the whole
universe of me. wait, just one universe, though,
not the brightest or most unique, but mine, distorted
by some lump with the gravitational attraction of a hundred
collapsed galaxies. that is what draws me to darkness.

1997: now, all I would have to do is miss a turn
while bicycling down the mountain at 60 miles an hour.
it would be ecstatic for sure to step out of the body
for a moment at speed, touching rocks and rolling down
the rocks and stopping lifeless cradled by rocks.
but I am skilled at riding and arrive in balance again.

1998: have to listen to dreams. dreams show me different
ways, slow ways that are the result of quiet desperation taken
to slow conclusion. i see myself slowly drowning in the ocean;
i swim until i can swim no more. too tired to struggle,
even to fight the water in my lungs. just welcome it and sink
and let the eyes grow dim and let the brain shut down—
the brain, that hysterical organ that seems to be the source
of my imbalance, of my inability to be at peace for very long.
once it is gone ... but then all the rest will be gone too
and no one will mourn, only wonder where i am.
and wonder and wonder until they die too, never knowing,
but never willing to know completely ...

1999: i know now that it is simple. that i just stop eating.
let the pain overwhelm me for a moment, but not doubt
the resolve not the intent. once past the pain
i can watch and feel the changes as things shut down to rest.
the flesh slowly melts away. the mind becomes clear;
the focus on the heart as it slows, as muscles become fuel
for this last muscle between me and purity. the purity
of the bones, the skull, the meat sloughed off, sloughed too
the concern for the longings of the meat and all its desires.
the simple beat that ends in nothingness. what could be
more simple, what more pure? the beat stops, but
the music of the atoms, of particles in a field of waving grass—

no the grass is just more particles dancing in the emptiness,
and the music continues as long as any thing moves.

2001: now this would make a romantic conclusion.
the answer to the question posed by the betrayal of love;
the appropriate gesture, the wasting away at the final loss
of dreams. but if the love is lost so easily, at the flick
of a pen, or the lust for another, then it is trivial
and cannot sustain the path of passing. it passed.
let it pass without my passing too. it cannot be
a reason; it cannot dissuade me from the path
from dreams to nothingness, yet.

2003: after normal years, another opportunity. tragedy.
but her tragedy, not mine. i understand and can change
and therefore cannot be tragic. nevertheless, i open
the hospital window and rehearse carrying her
in my arms as we drop eighteen stories to the concrete
pad below. i visualize it; her suffering over, unconsciously;
mine ended by will, but i cannot do it. i will not alter
her path, or mine, though either be far worse.

2004: a year. a chance to swim to nowhere. but i must
fast before going. not knowing for sure. desperate to avoid
some accident driving or flying. my spirit has been scattered
these past two years to the trees. what if they don't ever
want to give it back? would it be better in trees?
it cannot matter. so, i go on longer, sucking in experiences
and toying with them in the emptiness of my mind, wondering—
but knowing it cannot go on that much longer. the body
has its own pace and rate of change, as does the mind.
now, i'm thinking of ways to kill myself, that are more
interesting, when a window salesman calls to urge
me to improve my house. but, this house is where
i could die! i must have it for another year.
but then i remember that here is not the place.
the sea is the place—so that i can never be discovered,
so the mystery is as complete at its end as it was
at its beginning. i say no thanks and hang up.

idiot with ferns

solid things sublimate, then blow away
and dreams precipitate in pools and pools
evaporate from clay that cracks under
the heated breeze.
i've already told you how the breeze
follows me into the room at night
and how the window keeps presenting
vistas in a different foreign light.

i'm an idiot with ferns by the way
but prefer the tempo of plants.
the light bulb is buried by day;
ants visit the refrigerator.
i colonize the kitchen, paving the plastic tiles
with dedication, combating the mouse
of ideas with the charm of repetition.
words nibble at thoughts replaced by the smell
of iron pots and tea whose presence casts shadows
more colorful than words into the dream.

neutral beauty

Empty white plastic grocery bags, like self-directed
balloons, rise gracefully above the asphalt lots
and express the intent of the moving air,
itself careless about what it carries
with heat-island lifts and back-alley currents,
dust, leaves, feathers, souls, cupped plastic
it does not matter; there is no logic to expression,
no limit to what may exhibit beauty,
yet without the air under it, like any beauty.
it can contribute to entropy,
to suffering and destruction, smothering fish
or trapping birds to drown.

three wildernesses

1. i picked berries, knowing more would grow,
and went on, never looking back
to see if anyone followed,
but i knew they would,
in legions.
    green things growing wild, trails always new;
the trees cast shadows so long
it took a day to pass through.
somewhere in the forest a vision came
stopped in sifted sunlight spread his arms and disappeared.
    i dropped my kit by unnamed flowers
and lay on the cool moss: this wilderness was mine
no one would enter here but me; travelers
looked, passing by but kept on for their own horizon.

2. i bought an apple at the grocery for some coins
and moved back into the crowds on the morning sidewalk.
asphalt streets in lines, some trees in shadows from buildings
in the sun. it took an hour of buses to reach home,
that uniquely numbered combination of building blocks
at intersections and rooms on numbered floors.
    i set my briefcase on the carpet stretched out on an unmade
bed and looked at a wilted plant: i thought this place
a wilderness and no one ever entered here;
people looked passing near, briefly, from their hurriedness.

3. i thought of fresh fruit and wondered where it grew
or if i could get there. i had come late to the earth,
after it had been stripped bare
from all the hungry years before.
    what wonders held the ground i did not know.
i searched the clouds of memory and found a wilderness
waiting: pieces from passages in books
and half-forgotten photographs; i gained
a vision of the mountain and tastes from a hidden
fountain: birds, trees, scurrying sounds—all that i had hoped
for and expected—a separate virgin planet with its own
imaginary sun, a cave, primeval well, crystal life

in its own cell:
this is the last wild place no one comes in or out,
no one even cares about this end of the wild universe.

three prisons

1. eaten by a bamboo dragon captured by teeth and claws
and thrust down the throat to lie in humid darkness
bamboo walls and vines iron stand with porcelain bowl
a dirt bed with rags that scatter when I wake
exercise and clean memorize the grains
repetition without end
all life entertains
changing guards changing seasons changing me

2. another day and all night long with no place
to lie down open to air and water waiting for the light
sleeplessly rain here travels sideways from the ocean
through the trees through the ventilators
in the mens room door, bringing the coolness
of night under flat fluorescent light, paper towels
on tile paper towels for covers scatter when i wake,
stretch out concrete ache, check for roaches
or false dawn and try to sleep again.
it's worth it for the sand and sun.

3. pride and disappointment share the patchwork bath
and room with a kitchen on the stairs. forty watts above
my head brings out the sculpture in old plaster;
dirt seems natural. i finished trying to read and went to bed,
a single mattress dropped between the stove and wall,
warm with all my clothes on. ceiling rat patter
lullaby to sleep with no dreams.
pigeons coo morning from the roof and under peeling eaves.
i watch sunlight fill the corners through cellophane
stuffed broken glass bathroom windows
and make shadows from ruined furniture—must escape.

howard the janitor's daydream

unbeknownst to anyone i am the greatest swordsman
in the world though i make my living with a mop.
when everyone leaves and shadows grow
i listen look carefully about and stop—whip around
and catch them sneaking up—turn aside their blades
and set, slash the air before their faces
laugh the shadows are no match. i lunge and parry,
lunge and stab and the evening has begun.
through hundred-watted corridors three-feet wide i gain
the ground taken by surprise. oh, faithful bucket, sturdy
friend, we've been had, we've been trapped, led
before a raft of men without reaching julianne.
what awful torture must she endure if we are caught
and cut short?! ah, well, enough, kick and up two stairs
engaging left, engaging right,
steel sparks on blades well met.
grim cacophony, noisy knife! there, you bucket, distract
these knaves with slosh of water, tinny wheels
while i race up the spiral stair to reach
the tower vault remote.
i've caught a guarding ear these yokels know
i'm here they've sealed off the board room but i kick
the door aside! ahh, captains chairs and
floorlamps, dwarfs before the sword,
but time, they trade their lives for minutes, do i hear
a scream, a moan? a voice that's angry
with command? will i never reach
the chamber that keeps my innocent jullianne?
chairs succumb to precision broom
as i clear the last away! hermann! ha!
the challenge laid
the door is wide, the bed displayed,
squat cyclops, choose your grave!
i charge without a pause, fall before
a cunning table but as slow motion
begins i throw a dusty rag to block
his eye and rolling, stab the screen, pull
the plug and—

"*what?!* what the *fuck* you doing?!"
"well, i, i saved your li—"
"*plug* the teevee in! or i'll *miss* the ending;
and *pick* up *that table*!" spoke sweet julianne.

the garden of pain
my life is uneventful—a sop to promise,
a symphony of innocence until destroyed
by the constant addition of random noise:
eat, sleep, drink, excrete, and repeat.
stand, futilely, as gravity draws us flat.
storms allow no dignity, unanswered
questions leave no meaning; quantity
is monotony; occasional light radiates away.
there is no heroism in being full,
no failure in emptiness, no honor
in duty, no purpose in living, no—

the world is not dedicated to saving beauty,
life is not preparation for death, the whole
is not made to last, the song not saved
for the end. the boredom of life,
for moments, is replaced by the suffering
of being. but what fine, ripe fruits
are produced in this sad fallen garden.
all the pain of our lives, unseen beneath
the skin, fills to fruition and bursts
at death—
wet seeds flung in the air—

the weed of nonattachment
feasting on the weed of nonattachment
i made a desert of tropical splendor
passing by the fruits of listening i spoke
to hear my own sound
burning the weed, every touch a torrent of pain,
intolerable, fascinating
focusing on the strangely minute the world
passes by in a blur
i leap past, i bend in and away to nothing,
consumed by the weed.

quelling the rat of desire
doing dishes one night i saw the awful
shadow reflected on the faucet,
i felt the teeth tear my throat and rip
my flacid carcass. visions uncontrolled kill
when the gift descends.
Then the regret of life, its other side, rises
to light and cannot be denied so i accept,
but dread the shade i cannot control and wish
for the woman i cannot hold.
ah, visions are inspired as they are withheld
and i accept the paradox that I must create alone
and die in the jaws of the rat of desire.

the victim lucid under the light of torture
there are only certain things you—
pain is of another world this body will disintegrate
in time, without your help—
smear my lips with shit it's easily washed off again
and i find no threat in tasting
what you body couldn't use—
cut me, unzip my precious skin or burn openings
red with pain lost from another world—

it will grow together again in time
crush me, i will not bring children to such misery.
i knew love, it is enough to have memories
you cannot touch.
you took my eyes, my ears and proved
to me your strength and now i cannot move, cannot—
everything turns over—
pain escaping from all bounds i will not be saved, no
i will not say who, but will die quietly, secretly afraid
now you will bear my seed that will grow inside you
not seeing it or feeling it and not knowing for sure.

monsters

monsters inhabit grocery stores spilling sugar in the aisles
with their need for sweetness
they are always hungry and they have high ambitions
no matter what the prize
monsters occupy positions that used to go to those
who would try a little harder to be human
but monsters have the documents and they do the hiring
and guard the sty with care
they host symposia over ball game scores
and drink to superfluity;
their pedagogues misguide
they fill the void of possibility
and permit no other vacancy
they crowd the halls and galleries
monsters raise their salaries
and campaign against the waste and pests and weeds
bodies under tubes and sheets the anatomy
of feeling withers on the table
through all our misfortunes green articulated fingers
point the way to being complete

killer

i waited, waited, my lust is sated by blood of fated
innocents slated to leave life.
i stopped, listened, rainpools glistened,
footsteps quickened
dark streets thickened like fresh mud.
horrid fear and scalding tear stand
very near planned
not to hear hand on my knife.
i cursed and cursed streetlights dispersed
my web so immersed
in darkness rehearsed for his blood.
i ran ahead low in shadows spread
so thin my thread—no
closer his tread—oh damn this lot!
he stopped but under light, afraid of thunder
darkness alike, i wonder
when he'll blunder from his spot.
theater at an end or waiting for a friend
for dinner to spend
more money and mend sore gripping thirst.
oh, come walk gladly and greet me sadly
who wants so badly
to murder you madly— quench mine first!
i slipped closer grimly past shadows cast dimly
by lamp-posts
set thinly on paths lined simply with white mist.
i struck his head, caught him dead, sand
where he bled spanned
darkest red land with his gore.
gorge me lust i thrust and thrust,
my blade turned rust, lie
with him in dust why cut him more!?
i robbed his corse tried laughing
voice hoarse, felt no remorse,
die renewing the source, my life from his!

lessons in anonymity

fail at the expectations of others.
do not do anything fast. do not advertise
yourself, or sell. forget the importance
of names; know individuals. claim nothing—
accomplish less. be useless.
be part of everything else.

be full.
be whole and regard the flow
of wind and water. be wind and water
and flow. sit quietly doing nothing.
be yourself.

conceal yourself in the open
and remain unknown. leave nothing
for your children; have no children.
leave no trace for history.
no one will know whether or not you existed.

the importance of being slow

if you're fast, there's always someone faster
but if you're slow, it really doesn't matter.
if you're fast, there's always someone to beat
but we who are slow have no reason to compete.

being slow means that everyone can catch up
and nothing really passes by unnoticed.
there is nothing that cannot be grasped
eventually; nothing escapes our slow attention.

slowness adds another whole dimension
offering time to see what waits to be seen
the large and small and connections between,
the lamp-post and star, a worm under bark.

deserted buildings

after the inhabitants leave
the furniture is taken first. then
attachments are subtracted
until the building is a thought
nowhere supported, empty light.
            stripped to bare geometry
and cambrian components. the beams
stand like palisades ready to rejoin
the ground. no glass is left; shadows
curl where human activities never met.
    a vision unfolds like a jonquil
of men in an earlier age fitting bricks
in straight, lined rows and laboring
up the stairs—gone, now, there
are zigzags on a wall leading
neither up nor down.

            the skeleton cannot turn
to the moon, as a growing carrot can.
it stands in a vanished perspective.
there is a proper scale, not too far
to not see, nor close enough to hear
the chorus in a crystal lattice of iron.
the ruin takes place in a flatscape
of the mind, unrecognized.

potato woman

the reporter noted that she stood waiting
on the wooden porch, a tuber of flesh.
he walked up the muddy path and her muddy
features presented themselves: incredibly
blue eyes abandoned in a wasteland
of malnutrition gripped by oily strands
of hair. he had heard about her garden
(another filler, human interest angle).
what did she do? just grow vegetables.
why live out here alone? she was poor,

no one wanted to live with her, her children—
would she share her garden secrets?
well, she just put seeds in the earth,
didn't do much, just watched them grow, watched—
no, he didn't need to see the garden, just thanked
her and left to type it up.
her neighbor thought she had the shape of a pear—
no, the shape of a rosebud
waiting warmth and sun to unfold;
she had had too many winters; her eyes hibernated
in disinterest of possessions, but she
understood the seasons; often the wise
have the appearance of imperfection, useless
for human purposes. the story was forgotten;
she died, but will be carried on, in trees
and flowers, in squirrels and deer, for she
was kind and cared for living beings.

the prophet of beauty
i am not a prophet, i celebrate waste.
everyone admits that beauty is truth but when
is truth not beauty, when can you separate
the two with separate tastes?

waste is a failure of imagination.
regard nature: from clouds of frosty hydrogen,
stars are just the burning refuse of atoms condensed
in space. once gods turned heroes into stars;
we turn ours into waste disposal kings.
our atmosphere came from the waste
of volcanoes and cooling condensations; oxygen
is exhaled by plants from carbon dioxide,
then breathed by animals. monoxides,
freons collect— waste in quantity breeds
its own solution.

narrow vision cuts through the web of relations;

the world adjusts to a touch, and every action
has its cost in some reaction, nothing
can be discarded and not return; everything
can be used if only you know how.
waste is the generic term for
all the things we cannot use;
beauty is the waste we keep
to balance all the things that we abuse.

the principles of farming

your tears could make the desert bloom—
you had what you desired, but fed it to greater
desires. you were born with these:
rock, clouds, and rivers, fertile flower-clad
soil, locust, antelope, and lion. the grasses
that held your world together supported the wandering
herds and predators but were plowed under
by human economics.
we must have land that we can own we will work
our hands to bone will learn the rhythms
of the years and plant what grows best here
round and round and round we plow
then fertilize and weed by plane— we would plow
by plane if we could— then wait until the season gives
we must produce and reproduce that everyone
may have enough and more, we grow a pleasant surplus
for this earth is a fertile wife
we must grow and reproduce, reproduce
and grow; the land has more to give.
farming is the heart of civilized life
there is a myth among farming people of unlimited
growth and health what have we lost because of it?
follow your breath to the clouds
and follow the tracks in the dust.

arson

i have always loved flowers and trees that bore fruit;
i waited with the green for colors to come and carefully
cut down the ones too old to prune.
there are places in the city too long untended—
it has always been fire that kept the trees in trim
and burned away the trash to strengthen the wild forest.
is fire not the fruit of iron become too ripe in houses?
are seeds not spread in smoke to clear the tangled
growth and give architecture change?
is fire not the wood in bloom?

nemesis

we fear the food we take from the sea; we fear
the grain we grow in fertilizer. we fear
the air that we breathe, we fear
the water that we reuse
after it has cooled steel and flushed away
our waste—we fear the ghosts
of ourselves, cast away in chemical drums,
and all the beings that we have wronged;
we fear the harm may be returned,
so we keep their numbers down and sterilize
our drinks and dirt.
we fear our overconfidence, blind
and immoderate, ignorant of what remains
in the dark, knowing everything is dark.
we fear the vacuum in the hearts of our young,
whom we educated without mercy to support us
in our deserving age. we fear to stop.
we cannot stop, but cannot not stop.

lessons in synergy

at the edge of newark, wastes are dumped.
trucks discharge their mixed refuse
by the side of the pond.

gravity sorts the load as it rolls
down the slop; the paper drops out
and tires roll to the bottom.
bacteria decomposes the middle level
to strange combinations of materials;
methane seeps the ignites the heart.

with food, heat and information
rats breed.
the new masters of the planet:
from what unborn,
even the death of ice hides.

mirrors

a mirror is a rectangle of silver or crystal
connected to an image through nonexistent
space by rays of light whose angles of reflection
all are equal. any smooth surface or polished metal.
it must be neutral to trust. mirrors reflect
no character. socrates was ugly anyway;
descartes was just as vain;
whitehead smiled just the same.
mirrors are brittle and cold. they cannot reflect
desire. shakespeare wanted money, mozart handsome
clothes; einstein time to think
and contemplate the sea.
polished metal, leaded crystal, every word,
every science, every stillness is a mirror, water
that is clear, a mind reflecting,
the world—the glass of all is all.

crystal skull
the shell once profaned by flesh is bare
the meat long served to other beings.
the heat has all dispersed and ice alone
remains seen.
it is ice that reflects our interest
ice that holds the vacuum that holds all light.
the sockets stare but invite inspection,
threaten extinction—even crystal faces dissolution.

souvenir
she watched them for several days carefully working
on the house removing white siding, dismantling
the chimney, taking up oak flooring.
one morning the house was gone and under clouds
of dust a bulldozer loaded trash, broken plaster
and lathing on a truck.
the woman slowed her grocery cart, left it
and cautiously approached
the emptied foundation; she stretched
and reached for a small slat,
struck the ground twice with it and smiled.

the flatscape of philosophy
the flower of ideas wilts
when torn from the stem
so paper flowers are made to hold their shapes
longer for display—they never fade,
but they do not build soil or attract moths
and bees. the pudgy men sit comfortably
fashioning paper flowers fastidiously
in a smiling garden, filling the silence
with wagner.

an offering for godel

the poem: x

the solution: $x = 1^{20} * 2^8 * 3^5 * 4^0 * 5^6 * 6^9$
$* 7^{18} * 8^5 * 9^0 * 10^9 * 11^{19}$
$* 12^0 * 13^{20} * 14^8 * 15^5 * 16^0$
$* 17^{23} * 18^{15} * 19^{15} * 20^4 * 21^0$
$* 22^9 * 23^{14} * 24^0 * 25^2 * 26^{12}$
$* 27^{15} * 28^{15} * 29^{13}$

givens: letter order: t=1, h=2, e=3, ()=4 ...
letter value: a=1, b=2, c=3, d=4 ...

where: (letter order)$^{\text{(letter value)}}$

in: the fire is the wood in bloom

the use of books
el greco sat at the heavy oaken desk.
fresh ink was transferred in silence
to the crumpled parchment, experience
layered thickly with thought
and bound in leather.

after fifty years five volumes of his
philosophy. the books were kept in
the glass-front case by the fireplace
in the study—they were there
when he died in his sleep.

his nephew knelt on a grassy knoll
at night, making rocket caps of parchment—
a spark, the trail sheds its verbal embrace
and suddenly thought is returned to light
the system complete.

transtemporal telephony

your local telephone company is pleased to announce
its new, transtemporal dialing system!
another first! for you!

here is how it works: just dial one, then—
and here is where it's different!—
the year month day and time, then the area code
and same old number. your phone company automatically
calculates the past coordinates of the galactic arm
and beams the message back to you!

difficult? yes, but only for us and we do the work!
and best of all! those old telephone books
that you saved for so long still are good—
try it! call someone!
were there conversations left unfinished? feelings
unexpressed? unrequited love?
misunderstandings uncorrected, left hanging? call
back now, you've no excuse!
everyone's away from you? at a loss for friends?
remember when you had them? call them back! now!
forgotten what happened? what you did then? call
yourself and find out!

follow these simple rules: sorry, no collect calls allowed.
payment in advance for total time consumed—
it's how we pay for our research— remember,
we're working on the future!

"sir, that was 30,782,545 minutes. please deposit
111,127,732 quarters, 167 dimes, 1 nickel, 3 pennies ..."
"maybe that postage stamp i bought in 1958—get
a message back to mom, have her call collect ..."

reading meters

a famous medium: "most of the time, i don't feel
anything, but sometimes when the energy rises
i see silver coins stuffed in little steel boxes
pregnant with anticipation for the bent collectors
who take their charges to some higher destiny.
i have esp with parking meters and vending machines;
i can tell when they're full or when they're jammed.
i can see the evil ones, with grey metallic auras
or the good ones ringed with sky blue and cloud white.
i have sympathy with mechanical contraptions.
you always know when your parking meter is up
if you have clairvoyance toward machines—"

then she said: "god doesn't care, for the good
of meterkind, for justice and mercy in vending—
slugs abound, crowbars kill, and when electricity
fails—but i can read vibrations from discontented
switches and notice aluminum's resentment,
violation pending—oh, pray, pray! to goldberg
and ford, the gods of assembly, for an end
to mechanical anguish! Pray now! You, pray!"

the stone

dark empty branches wave at windows
the glass is old and thick in places
and magnifies some of the lines
so that houses and streets enter in waves,
old and bent by the light.

the chalk dust settles, diagrams
of inscrutables remain—the gaunt
head nods. tired light falls to dust.
he is sealed in custom. smooth cracks
and all the colors turn to grey.

he cannot find it though he has plumbed
the depths—a most precious thing with no
value, it lies in the waste of the world,
an unknown thing known to all—magic
like a grain of sand that contains
the universe—it lies waiting.

the grey man bends over grey bread,
the crumbs spread like grains of sand.
thought digests the body. he gathers
the crumbs, lacking only a spark to fuse
the sand to glass and look through.

he sweeps the crumbs to the floor
and stands, scratching more signs
on the blackboard. the stone rests
in the chaos of dust on the floor.
incandescent light leaves the window.

retreads
where the inflated dreams that carry us
on the road to progress hit the asphalt
of reality and fall apart

obvious truths too
entertainers are far more valuable than
the people that they pretend to be.

people who play for a living are praised far more
than those who work to keep the exchanges moving.
and the dirtier the work, the less desirable tasks,
the more needed, the less romantic.

nature whole is useless, nature complete has no value,
but nature diminished must be miniaturized
and preserved.

clever prophecies of henry d. thasinger, 1917-1999
anything can be reduced and figured out; then
we can remake anything and get it to work.

anything that can be cooled and miniaturized
can be controlled more efficiently.

we need not worry about resources on earth.
we can make everything from hydrogen and energy.

humans are basically the same and have the same
basic needs. with education, we will all recognize this
and live peacefully in perfect harmony

if we provide the possibilities for everyone,
people will always work hard and make the right
choices to maximize their lives.

zen of baseball

i bought a baseball bat yesterday, a slugger, wooden,
painted black—i'm applying it to everything i bought
for you: the cello, stained glass, tables—
too bad it won't work for your clothes,
i'll need gasoline and tar for those, and gasoline for
your awful novels, that had none of the overwrought
 passion or stupid naiveté of your diaries.

oh, how could i have been so stupid, so naive myself
to believe that you wanted to only be a nun,
that you didn't want physical congress with anyone.
of course, your affairs must have been as limp
and bloodless as our phone calls. all you did was talk
and dream, idolize and fantasize.
you mentally masturbated over yourself so much,
pulling your face into tight contortions
then photographing it to pretend you just had plastic
surgery, that you had no time or need for physical
contact, except to hear compliments about how good
you looked for a fifty year old woman. my oh my.
that's all there is to life—a compliment from a younger
man? maybe you should have had children;
the meaning might have been enough for you to forget
yourself, the you who was always held in the forefront
of every activity, the sole heroine of every story.

i'll need bullets and bombs to destroy every life
you touched instead of mine, every ear that heard a lie,
every eye that saw you, every nose that sniffed
your expensive perfume or soaped belle chose. Every
neck twisted, every car burned, every building
you were in, leveled, every city, every airport, everything
burned and scattered. now that would be more
impressive than some weak compliment given
by a desperate male mouth to a desperate female ear
ending in a dry quick entry, then vacuous diary
entry. burn the birth control pills, the urinary infection
pills, the sleeping pills, the prozac, all the other

pills, that confused you—

'it's not my fault,' i hear you say. Even in that you echo
your simpering ridiculous father. you made yourself
depressed then hoped chemicals could raise you,
then used them as an excuse to be foolish.
burn the guideposts for your adventures:
a book on "the rules" for how to get a man by not
returning phone calls for three days. did it work
on the architect? no. did it work on fat nat? no, i guess
not. tear up advice from your single girl friends
who do not know how to keep a man past a one night
stand? did you try that? did that work? i guess not. rid
the world of the overused shakespeare you used
to impress men, or the cat you bought
to take for walks so men—well, vain eric anyway—
would talk to you about your mutual kindness
for animals.

i'll need nuclear weapons for the memories—servicing
some blubbery gimp once a month then waxing overripely
about it on paper is not an adventure or a perilous
new world. maybe if you had learned to masturbate,
you might have kept your pallid dreams consistent
and less messy. you praised your new expensive love, but
was my love for you less—in its purity and faith,
in its unflagging devotion and support? its sheer passion
and depth that must have frightened you back
to fantasies. can it compare with a weak little tumble
on the bland canvas of your mythology? was it stronger
than a real body, real mind, passionate fluids?
that's it? a false solipsism that wandered off on its own?
some adventure. how sad. now your life is simple,
your brain damage extreme and each moment is forgotten
as you live it. your accident left you just for me.
is that what is left for me? you? the diminished version?
that no one visits or writes or dreams of—
oh, good. i still have the bat. maybe i'll just play baseball—
it's what a buddhist would do.

personal ads for intellectuals

multiversant genius seeks quaesitum to share mirabilia;
no sophomaniacs or cacophrenics need answer.

dilection with practical knowledge of effleurage,
philematology, melliloquy, and silence desires
equal sarmassophile for epithymetic time.

nephologist seeking eidolon, gelastic dreamer
looking for alterity.

call me to let me worship at your penetralium
tempean peri seeks strong philocalist

nemophilous biologist seeks someone
with ramage for physiolatry

personal ads for sensitive others

swm, mature yet young, rich yet environmentally concerned,
serious but playful, seeks set swf. send clipped bill.

reagonomics victor with big portfolio looking to trickle down
on your station; if interested, bring matches & altimeter.

looking for a man who likes to laugh and dance,
is independent and is willing to share me with stuffed animals.

i want sex. call me

millionaire watching

good times watching teevee, at least until hank
opened his big mouth and told me that the average pay
for shot was eight thousand dollars hit or miss,
play or not. after that, it was hard to root for anyone—
even the underdogs made seven.

that's all we see anymore, millionaires playing ball,
or millionaires pretending to be cleopatra or joe louis,
or millionaires playing or telling us how much
we can help their businesses.
millionaires at work, millionaires at war
millineries at parties, millionaires at home millionaires
with children—we only tolerate them because we want
to become them.

ambiguous service announcements

"serving the older battered woman"—
a conference on deep frying them
and how to present the meat
and what side dishes to offer

"elder abuse program"—
the official state course
on how to abuse elders
reach limits without getting caught

"meals on wheels"—
peace corps volunteers
on roller-skates serve urban cannibals
a feast in londonderry—
the skates can be reused.

the mathematics of homelessness

$$34549192 = 0$$

bags of water

what happens when you are floating on the ocean,
or drinking water on a vessel?
is not a bag of water drinking water on a bag of water
on a bag of water?
skin stomach ship ocean-basin—just bags for holding water
things that keep you from combining
and losing yourself in the whole prematurely
and maturity is everything
water is the secret the solvent that keeps the soul
immersed in all after bags decay.

gotta get to hell on time

gotta get there fast
doesn't matter if i die because i'm going past
and it doesn't matter how
got to blow right by the law and pass every single car
in sight then speed up for school zones and drive on sidewalks
and if i crash or kill someone i just get there sooner
give way, get out, stand aside gotta get to hell on time
seek that warmer clime it's all right, it's a dry heat
and that certain torture the official loss of hope
gotta get there, gotta date can't be slow, can't be late
don't wanna pay the price no, no, he'll kill me twice
gotta get there fast everyone i know is waiting
so it can't be bad one more step,
then relax

equations of equality

poetry=weakness
fame=silliness
politics=cowardice
news=catastrophe
wealth=time
happiness=wine

49

Coyote Redivivus

the further frenetic mythopoetic adventures
of coyote in post-modern industrial civilization

Coyote cosmogenesis

First, nothing made water
then water made Coyote
then Coyote made water
then Coyote laid down and made land
he shit and made mountains
then he farted and clouds and air appeared
then he scratched his fleas and the land was populated
with fungus, plants, birds, animals, and people
then everything was ready for Coyote redivivus
Coyote redux,
Coyote man, Coyote woman.

And Coyote joyed in his world
mixing, testing, changing,
fooling around with every possibility,
every emotion, need, or wild idea,
taking them apart, recombining them,
interacting, interfering, entering
every play and event and scenting
it with Coyote odor, then sniffing,
sleeping, and dreaming—
what Coyote created at once
he destroys piece by piece.

Coyote invents television

Coming into the canyon surrounded by great rocks,
Coyote saw some children playing and figured
that they would want to play with him, but
he was wrong; they ignored him, and went on
running and hiding. Coyote thought, what kind
of game would they play with me, Coyote?

He went and found a cedar tree by the creek
and made a few beads out of its berries, colored
them with blue and yellow and put them on strings.
When he saw the children again, he waved those
beads and spoke to them; they paid no attention,
acted like he was some kind of adult.

Coyote did not like this; he needed to be noticed
and laughed at. He went to a distant village
and traded water to tobacco woman for tobacco
(he knew it will not rain and she could trade with
corn man). Back in the canyon that evening he made
a fire, waited for careless children.

When he saw them he lit his pipe and waved
it at the children, saying, "Look here, big fire, smoke,
great fun." But they continued their running game,
and as Coyote watched and smoked voluminously
his tail swept into the fire and ignited—he yipped
knowing they must have smiled.

It was not enough. So, he traveled to a far distant village
of the people colored like ashes. He made a thing those
kids could never resist. He paid for help with promises
of fame, knowing the bargain was good (fame is
nothing). He put it in a mysterious box and carried
it for many weeks and for miles.

Now at their own village, he tapped the current of
the earth, displayed the box at the edge of the well.
It was on when the children came out of their hogans
and they sat down beside the triumphant Coyote.
Then they all watched in silence together as
the Roadrunner left Coyote in the dust . . .

Coyote steals a car

Hundreds of nights had passed, and Coyote lay
bathed in the gently flashing, funny, light
of the magic box. Time for another snack
he thought and rolled over for corn chips.
No chips left; the children had gone he noticed,
tapping his belly with a dirty nail.

His belly trembled and kept shifting, then fell
to the side and raised a little dust. This is
odd, Coyote thought. How did this happen?
He stood and his belly bounced on the ground.
He fell over again and pushed it, poked
it, pressed it, played with it like a new toy.

The next day he went to see Gila monster,
who was lying on the sand in the sun,
thoughtfully tapping his own belly. "Look,"
Coyote said, and swung his belly over
his friend. In the shade, Gila nodded,
"What a fine belly, how can you carry it?"

Coyote flopped on his side, with his nose
near Gila's nose. Both exhaled for a while.
Coyote spoke slowly, "I cannot lose it, but
it is too heavy to carry very far—I will not
be able to chase any food or visit anyone."
    Then Gila spoke, "why not get a car?"

They stood watching the highway. The cars
were too fast to catch, they agreed. "I know
where they nest," Gila said. That night,
Coyote couldn't decide, so many choices:
mustangs, vipers, pintos, jaguars, dusters,
then he saw it—the Plymouth Roadrunner!

Getting in was easy, The windows were open,
but turning the key—had to use his teeth.
Then he had to open the door for Gila
who said he knew how to do the things
on the floor to make it go. Then it did go,
a dark shape flying through the night.

Coyote grinned and howled with delight,
he pointed it down the darker ribbon, head
outside in the rushing air, Gila on the pedal
asking what was going by. Then Coyote saw
a mouse and turned the car to follow it.
The car bounced over sandy ridges.

Gila was bounced off the pedal. The car stopped
in the sand. Gila got back on, but the wheels
only spun. After digging in a while, Gila left.
Listening to the engine rumble, Coyote howled
with frustration, then sighed, dialed for heat,
curled up in the seat and went to sleep.

Coyotes faces Godzilla or Yippi yi yi

The car was too hot during the day, but gave
a nice shadow, so Coyote lay underneath it.
Having stolen a car, heck, having even stolen
the sun once, Coyote needed a new challenge
but what? That would take a lot of thought.

So he thought, ate, thought, slept, thought,
thought, thought, ate, ate, slept, thought
and the desert moved around him
the cholla bloomed and the pear
but nothing bloomed in Coyote's head.

Too much work, he decided, best to eat
and sleep some more and see if ideas
would come when he wasn't looking
but the ideas were buzzing around
different heads elsewhere in the desert.

Coyote was irritated by the mouse
whose hole he was resting over
so he decided to teach the mouse
a lesson and eat him. He dug down
then to the right, then the left, down.
Where was Badger when he needed help?

Mouse said, "Wait! What are you doing?"
"Just hanging around for dinner," said Coyote.
Mouse warned him, "Better not stay here,
the giant who kills everyone will see you."
"Oh, I'm not afraid of giants," Coyote boasted,
"why, I'd kill him if I saw him. Fix his wagon."

"He's closer than you think, bigger than
you imagine," Mouse replied, "you might need
a really big stick." Coyote bared his teeth
and held up a paw, "See these," he said,
"these can cause pain in mice and men.

Look!" and Coyote danced the fighting dance
swinging wildly at shadows, hitting himself.
Mouse snuck off while Coyote was bragging.

Maybe Mouse was right, Coyote thought,
maybe there were beings with powers
greater than his. He saw a stick and picked
it up. I could hit him with this, finish
him before—where was the mouse?

But the Mouse was watching from
the saguaro on the hill, having left
through the back door. Coyote was
still five feet from the door and looking
dusty and hot. He snuffed at the dirt.

It was getting hotter, but then a good
cloud made shade and he started
digging again. Part of the cloud
pointed at the mountains. No, the shade
was *from* a mountain. Coyote looked up

and saw a giant Gila monster, something
too big, too unnatural—Coyote dropped
his stick, yipping pathetically, tail tucked
he blazed a trail east, not looking back;
maybe it was just a bizarre shadow
cast by a mouse, but maybe it was better
to come back and find out later . . .

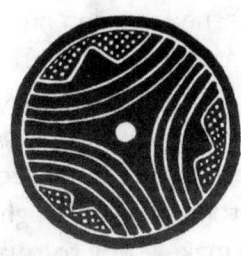

Coyotes goes nuclear

The shadow had scared him he could admit;
he was quivering like an agave worm,
even if he was not sure what it was
exactly, a Gila monster larger than oak trees
larger than boulders and some mountains.
If it came back he had to have protection,
something that guaranteed his security
that is, if it wasn't his imagination.
What could hurt it? Large teeth or claws?
He had seen machines tear the earth with claws
large enough; he had to think. He slept.

It was cold again all night, he shivered.
Coyote had burrowed in the ground, but he got dirty;
he had used fire before and danced around it,
but that was too much work, all that wood gathering,
bending over, poking, getting more wood, feeding
the flames. There had to be a better way

He had seen the planes go over, these metal birds
of men, pushed by glowing branches,
carrying strange things from town
to town. He remembered where one had gone down
and burrowed in, and he could go there on his own
without the dance of badges and papers.

In a remote part of the desert, he found it,
half-buried. He dragged a long tube from the sand,
dragged it through the desert, for nights, then
buried it by a mesquite, next to den number 63.
It kept the den warm at night. Night after night
it was hot, and he could not get too close, so
he buried a bit away, behind a wall of sand.
He was warm, but then some fur and teeth started
to fall out. Must be getting old he thought,
have to find a woman, make a boy to carry on
the sacred traditions of being Coyote.

Coyote takes a mate

Coyote was running around one day, he ran
around from place to place, rock to tree, mesquite
to prickly pear, rubbing off his scraggly mangy painful
fur. Under the greasewood, he sat too tired
to move but itching.
                         "You need help," he heard
a voice say. He looked up and saw Mountain Lion.
draped across a limb. "What happened?" Lion asked.
        "I must be too hot." Coyote answered, "but water
doesn't help; soon, I'll be furless. Could you scratch
this?" he asked.
                         "No, I don't think so," Lion purred,
"but you could get a mate."
                                   A mate thought Coyote, rolling
over, that would solve everything. "Where would I start?"
        "Talk to Flicker," answered Lion, "he is always
nosing around into everyone else's business."

He knew there were females around. He had seen them
looking at him when he hunted and he watched
them back. "But watching won't get you a mate,"
Flicker said, "you need to woo a woman, make
her feel special, then pin her to the sand. For
a special price, I will set up a date and provide flowers
and sweet meats."
                         "Okay," said Coyote, "I'm game."
"Exactly," said Flicker, "sign here, initial here, piss there."

Standing in front of the clean new den, Coyote
was disgruntled; play the field, ha, all he had gotten
was dirty, have parties, ha, all he had gotten was used
for entertainment. The voluptuous Mole said that she
would mate with him, but had to have her own
den. Jacqueline Rabbit said she would mate with him
but she had to have willow to eat every day.
Ducky ignored him. He needed to try a new approach.
So he asked Kingfisher for help. Kingfisher said he knew

of a young female who lived by the flat mountain;
he would make arrangements. He did. On the right day
Coyote saw her by the streambed. She did not run away;
she stood by her prize, a mouse, backed up when
he approached and let him eat it; after several more,
he asked why, since he was older and slightly mangy.
She said she heard that he was a great explorer
(and thought he could be reformed into a good provider).
He thought she would be a good provider
and suggested that they hunt that night together.
They hunted together and traded fluids.
They decided to make a new den by the hill.
And his fur started growing back although
he remembered the glowing metal longingly;
but she would not hear of them living near it.

She wanted to get married, let some family and friends
see how happy they were. "I'll do all the work," she urged
and that was that. Soon the presents started arriving:
road runner traps, how to cook books—not funny,
those—even a cottonwood penis extender, which
disappeared immediately, and mice, many dead mice.

The ceremony was the very epitome of dignity,
promises were made, lies were exchanged, the bride
was dusted white, the groom's tail resined black.
Favors were traded for the banquet. The best animal
Raven forgot the ring, the maid of honor Badgera
went topless, the minister was drunk on berries.
Blackbird caught the bouquet and flew off.

Somehow they got back to the den. Coyote announced:
"Time for wedding night coyitus! It is the coynage
of the realm, coystyle!" He really wanted
to mate like a wolf, but couldn't get turned around
properly. Coyota didn't want her dust smudged, just
yet, so they lay back and barked at the moon,
yipped and barked, barked and yipped until
the sun rose and they sank into sleep.

Coyote gets analyzed

For weeks Coyote lay in the den, depressed. He no
longer admired his stomach, which had gotten bigger,
no longer lusted to speed through the night, was jittery
about large shadows from strangely shaped clouds, and
was always playing with a bald patch near his tail that
never grew back. He never wanted to mate, complained
Coyota, "Is it because I am fat with pups, your pups?"
Coyote groaned, more responsibility was looming.

Coyota told him there must be something wrong
he should be happy, now. Although he acted dignified
yet slinky sometimes, she was embarrassed to be with him
with her friends. He needed to see a specialist,
get better fast, maybe Desert insurance would cover it.

So they went to see Doctor Vulture, beneath the topless
yucca tree. "You know," the Doctor said, "I have helped
others worse than you—eagle for instance, who used
to skulk around eating dead cows—now look at him,
national symbol and all. Then there was Badger, soon to
represent a football team—"
                    "What about Rattlesnake?"
Coyota interrupted.
                    "Ah, that is a sad story, but with more
time, deeper analysis—but we want to help you now,
if you want to change."
                    "He does," said Coyota.
                                        "Well, let's begin,
eh?" Doctor Vulture leaned over, "do you love your mother?
Who was she?"
                    "The moon of course," Coyote said,
"How could anyone get warmth from the moon?"
                                        "Your father?" Vulture continued.
"Myth, hardly knew him, sprayed and ran."   The session
went for days, Coyota bringing them mice and water.

After a functional analysis of Coyote (Inputs: air, water, food,

dirt. Needs: warmth, others, victims. Outputs: saliva,
spunk, excrement), Doctor Vulture said it was common
treatable dual personality bipolar disorder, "Think," he said,
"you are revered as creator, great hunter, sacred supervisor,
and yet," Doctor Vulture paused, "as coward, thief, trickster.
This negative image is behavioral: From darting away at the first
sign of trouble, to eating other animals, or to eating anything."

    Coyotes muscles tensed to run, but Coyota leaned
on his foot.

      "You are burdened with the reputation of a greedy
bungler, easily duped by children or slow animals."

        "But wise enough to howl
at the approach of the unknown," Coyote added.

      "Hmm," said the Doctor, "you know, I rarely
give specific advice, but new ages require new sages, so
here goes: Act your age, you're about to be a father now
and cannot go trying to change your colors like bluebirds
or lizards. Don't get into trouble, think about your mate.
Ignore all the things you cannot change, move more slowly.
Give up your old sneaky friends like Raven and Snake, find
other couples with children. I would recommend that you get
the tail cropped and learn to stand and point, like a dog,
so that people will see your natural dignity. Gain a little
weight, like that stomach; and don't show your teeth."

Coyote lay where he was, slowly lifted his tail
and let it flow down again; it didn't raise any dust.
This is it, he thought, the end of exploration and excitement,
the end of life. Coyota nipped his tail and said,
"You can laugh, and things will flow and change themselves."

    Coyote yipped and laughed, ah, well, what else?
Then Coyota called him to dinner: Fruit from saguaro
and organ pipe cactus, like watermelon, a stinkbeetle
and blotched-lizard, with grasshopper mouse for desert.

Coyote plays dead

At first it was fun, the pups worshiped him, they gave
him their total attention, and he taught them to be
coyotes: When to yip, when to run, when to fight
(if your opponent was smaller and weaker), how
to find food, how to catch it (a decent five percent
of the time, although Coyota seemed to always near
thirty, bitch), how to keep it by not sharing—
he refused to vomit it back when they licked
the corner of his mouth—they needed to learn
dignity and self-reliance, too; even humans knew—

Then the dung and mucus, the barking and crying,
the lessons, the sheer responsibility of fatherhood
began to wear on him. He spent more and more
time with Badger and Rattler, playing games
of chance and losing his food. He searched
elsewhere for attention. Coyota spent time
with the girls, Skunka and Eagla, comparing recipes
and fur (or feather) patterns, the slatterns. The pups
were getting big enough to shake their toes after
they pissed on them. He felt less needed, unheeded,
depleted and unseated as master of his den, so
when should he leave and where should he go?
He needed to be appreciated, he wanted to be needed,
he needed a new challenge. He could help other
animals cope with the uncertainties of desert life,
the certainties of human encroachment on their
fair desert sandscape. That was it. He would do that,
he would, yes, he would; the Hollywood Arizona
desert community would have a new name, new
purpose, new error, er, era of prosperity and he
would be the be the looter, la, leader—

Then the pups jumped him and he played dead.
"Dad," they said, "tell us another story." He rolled
so his ribs sprang back and said, "We're going
to throw our spit in the ring. Play the politics game.

Denny, you get flyers—"
                              "What are flyers, dad?"
"Talking birds, you get them. Spotty, go get Badger.
Humpy, think about a campaign slogan—"
"It's Humphrey, Dad, and he's Spotsworth."
"—or a good lie, whatever."
And, Renren, stay between your mother
and me. C'mon, no more messing around. Let's go!"

Coyote runs for Mayor

Coyote said it was time to let Eagle retire, his ideas
were stale, his leadership weak. Animals were starving,
humans were racing around in mobile dens, killing
animal people and kidnapping cacti. Coyote offered
to feed all the animals and to protect the cacti.

The community met in the bottomland by the stream,
so all could drink peacefully while they talked, except
that Rattler swallowed a mouse before they began;
they made him cough her up and warm her until she
could breathe again. Rattler apologized with a hiss.

Peccary and Turtle wanted to run against Coyote. Eagle
saw the writing on the sand and withdrew as a lame
duck leader; he had ambitions beyond the stream anyway.
Each candidate was to give a speech
and then the community would vote. Coyote started,
the pups interrupting him with cheers and howls.
          Coyote said, "My platform is food for everyone."
If animals could not get enough food, he Coyote
would give each a mouse, except the mice,
who would each get a mushroom, that is, if
there were enough mice left to be hungry. Mouse
spoke up and said that Misses Mouse assured him
that they would outnumber everybody by next month
and could swing the election for some seeds and fungus.

Coyote coughed to cover up his swallowing Misses
Mouse whole, winking at Rattler. Then, Dung-beetle
spoke, saying that he could not use a mouse, but
sometimes more dung. And Bat spoke, saying
that he only ate mosquitoes. Coyote promised one
mosquito to each bat, but Bat replied that mosquitoes
were much lighter than mice, so he would need 97
mosquitoes a day. Coyote promised 98, but no one
thought he would ever catch enough for one bat,
much less the 6548 bats in the community. Coyote
was weak on math, about like a creosote bush.
The mosquitoes wanted a guarantee of two animals per night
to suck on; would Coyote be one? Coyote smiled weakly
and nodded. Coyota boffed his head sideways.

Peccary presented his platform, which was strangely
porcicentric. He spoke directly to the large animals—
wolf, cougar, bobcat, deer, and wolverine—suggesting
that humans were too good at hunting. To make
things more fair, he suggested making winter colder
or longer, with desert snow. All the large animals
agreed. Wolf suggested asking the small animals too
so when they asked great spirit, who made us, for approval,
they would have a stronger position.
                              Coyote sniffed
loudly, "He hasn't made anything easy for us lately,"
thinking 'I, Coyote, am a god. Did we suddenly forget that?'
But the other animals ignored him. So, they asked
opinions from Porcupine, Beaver, Mouse, Raccoon,
Martin, Bobcat, Jackrabbit, Frog, Turtle, Bat, Beetle, Mosquito,
Wren, Bee, Wasp, and some of the lesser, hard-to-see
or even hear insects.
                              Peccary repeated his strategy.
The large animals agreed, but the small were silent.
      Finally Turtle spoke: "That's good for you since you
have fur and fat, but we and the insects will get cold
and not be able to get food."
                              The large animals
liked Peccary's argument and wanted to go ahead.

then Turtle asked a pointed question: "If it is that cold,
and the berries freeze and plants die, won't you starve
in the spring? Of course, we small should survive because
we can eat bark and grubs underground." He banged
his head on his shell to show how serious he was.
The large animals were speechless.

                              Peccary admitted
that it made sense. He agreed to alter his promise
to limit cold weather to three months.
Now Turtle spoke his words slowly, and in fact many
of the animals entered a state not unlike sleep. Turtle
said he could not promise food for everyone, that
he could not change the weather, but he could
use common sense so that things were more balanced
in the whole desert ecosystem. He suggested sending
a group of representatives to Defenders and Greenpeace
to keep the mobile things, called 'bikes' or 'orvs,' away
from their homes. They would stress the value
of a clean healthy desert and the importance of all
the animals in the scheme of things. He suggested
allowing the status quo of eating and mating to continue
as it had in the past. Wolf hurrahed and thought
that they might take back some territory from the coyotes.
Turtle said he would appoint Peccary first as Vice
Mayor and include insects and mice on the City Council.
Coyote was so shocked he coughed up Misses Mouse,
who shook off the saliva and went off with Mister Mouse.
The community was pleased with the words of Turtle
and elected him as their Mayor.

Turtle said, "So it shall be: No pie-in-the-sky food
subsidies, no extended seasons. The animals can
go to their homes and the plants remain standing
or crawling." As Turtle walked by Coyote, he accidentally
butted him with his hard shell and stepped on
Coyote's tender pads with his nailed toes. Coyote yipped,
and Turtle said to the community, "How could you trust
someone who promises too much and then yips
at the slightest inconvenience."

                    Coyota had to lead
Coyote off before he tried to turn Turtle over and start
to eat his sweet meats. Coyote even growled
at Porcupine and Mosquito, but stepped on his own
tail and yipped. Things had gone well, he thought,
suggesting a re-election strategy to her.

Interludes

Coyote in the bag

Coyote was hungry. He had nothing left but his wits
and an empty bag. He had an idea. He threw in a few sticks
and blew in the bag. He went to where the Cactus mice
were playing. "What's in the bag, Coyotlbozho?" one small
mouse asked.
          "Songs, for dancing, but I can't reach them.
Can a few of you help me and carry them out?"
When five went in Coyote snapped the bag shut and ran
off. But he heard singing from the bag. One of the mice
was singing to cover up the sound of chewing.
Coyote put the bag down, when he looked in he saw
the twigs and a small hole. He snuffed the recent scent.
Rattlesnake smelled the scent also and came to the bag,
going in the hole. The mice snuck up and closed the hole.
The small one said "Coyotlyodel, we changed our minds
and came back for another song."
                              Coyote was puzzled,
since he knew there were no songs in the bag,
but he stuck his head in—

Coyote partnership stink

"Skunk, I need you to help me with a food problem.
You like mice?" Coyote whispered the plan in his ear.

Skunk slunk back to his underground house and lay down.
Coyote raced to the Mouse area and shouted, "It's Skunk,
he isn't moving, he may be dying! Please help, quickly."

The mice, who were generous and kind, raced
with him to the den.

Coyote said, "You push, I'll pull,"
The mice were relieved that he was in front. They started
lifting the striped guy and moving him up the tunnel.
Suddenly Coyote bit Skunk's nose and Skunk released
his scent, which caused the mice to swoon.

Coyote pushed by and gobbled six.
When he tried to get past Skunk again, Skunk said,
"where are mine?" and turned his weapon.

Coyote coughed
up three and said, "Just tenderizing them for you, heh, heh."

"This was a good idea," said Skunk between mouthfuls,
"let's get a larger meal."

"Such as?" Coyote wondered.
"Deer, deer are dumb," Skunk said.

Coyote liked this guy.
"Okay, look," said Coyote, "we'll just reverse the game.
Play dead here." and Skunk flopped down
and Coyote ran off to the deer tribe in the field.
"Help, Skunk has fallen and can't get up. I think he's dying."

A young fawn ran back with Coyote, the parents watching.
When they got to Skunk, Coyote said, "You push him back
to his den, I'll pull."

And it was bite, spray, eat all over again.
The partners were happy. But, Skunk had bigger plans,
"Let's try Bear."

Coyote shrugged, Bear was not the sharpest
pencil in the box, but his meat was strong.

They planned,
they executed, but Bear just sneezed and whupped
their scrawny butts—Although Mrs Bear found him hard to bear.

Coyote at bat

"Look out, Coyote, rancher is on the warpath," Bat whispered,
"seems he lost another cow when he came back after lunch."
  "Yea, I know," Coyote smirked, "he was out to lunch for six
months, one of the bovines tripped and landed on its head.
I had a small meal from him since he was dead, and hunting
wasn't that good. I may have left a footprint or tooth."
  "He's going to leave a poisoned cow carcass for you."
"Thanks, I learned better than Wolf."
                                              "But, Wolf didn't eat—"
"I Coyote triumphed due to excess and challenge.
Let Coyote eat the cattle and their cattle will become healthy.
Let him eat sheep and the sheep will benefit and thrive.
Rancher is stupid, unsuccessful. Coyote persists, prospers
and expands—"
                    "Which Coyote?"
                                        "I was just speaking
in the third-person, me, Coyote continues to live in the dreams
of his admirers as the primordial teacher—"
                                            "Who continues?"
"Never mind," Coyote sighed, "say, could you teach me
to hunt in the dark so no one could see me?"
                            "Sure," whispered Bat, "it's easy.
Here's the secret, as you run just make noise, a lot of noise,
and where the noise returns back to your ears, go
in that direction only. If you listen, you should be able
to hear the breathing of your prey. We'll try it tonight."

Later, that night, Coyote said, "Can you see the deer?"
"No, but I can hear it's echo."
                        "Whatever," Coyote sighed,
"can you point me and I'll start?"
                        Bat turned Coyote's head
and said, "Start running now! Straight ahead!"
And Coyote barked up a storm as he ran through the night.
Unfortunately, the deer was less dense than the saguaro
and Coyote brought down the cactus. He lay unmoving
and spoke to himself, "I am pierced. My head is split."

Coyote debates headsplitter

The setting: 'Coughing Eagle Memorial Puddle.'
The audience: Thirsty animals like Bobcat and Antelope.
"You know," Doctor Vulture commented, "the archetypal
trickster is closely associated with the devil. Perhaps
they are the same, particularly in Christianity, where the devil
is the embodiment of pure evil, the scapegoat for our
self-loathing. Beginning as a playful trickster, he put
on the mask of a Serpent and reasoned with Eve to try
a golden delicious."

Coyote ate a piece of corn tortilla.
Vulture continued: "Why Joseph Campbell described Coyote
trickster as a 'super-shaman' shaping the whole paleolithic
character. And Jung—"

"Doctor Vulture? Turkey Vulture? May I call
you Turkey? No? What is trickster but the hero of uncertainty,
the lover of ambiguity, and the creator of new ideas? Let us honor
me, umm the truckster, shower him, err me, with luxuries
and food. Let the paleolithic legend live in our hearts again!"

"As I was saying," Doctor Vulture emphasized, "Jung
considered, regarding Psyche, that the unity of nature was in
the middle, and trickster was the figure of unity, creating
harmony, metaphorically a trickster discourse, between—"

"Harmony?" Coyote interrupted, spraying tortilla chips.
"Here's your metaphor for harmony. I eat this corn,
I chew it and swallow it, then I sleep, then I shit, then I throw it
at your face, then I lick and smell it, and pronounce it good.
Your precious Jung also has argued that the trickster is
'undifferentiated energy' spinning through the universe, but I
focus my boundless energy on some poor sap, who has
to give me more food, so I don't have to run and chase it."

"Look at you now, you are posturing for the audience, trying
to entertain, while I, Dr. Vulture, articulate the laws of lying.
Listen! There are three problems with lying always. The first
is that your lies, which you meant to set you free
from the truth, can end up dominating you instead."

"So, what's
the problem, lies are lighter than truth and weigh less heavily

on the mind. Hey, dominate me."

"Well, another thing a life of deceit demonstrates is that eventually your lies catch up with you."

"No problem there either. I have plenty of time. If they catch up, I'll put them back in a bag," Coyote grinned.

Vulture was exasperated, "Finally, a trickster's deceitful ways teach us that in the end we only deceive ourselves."

"No problem again. Deceiving myself gives me pleasure and lets me abide with stinking reality. And at least I respect and love the deceiver. Deception keeps me healthy. I deceive myself that the sun is warm and loving and will not burn me, that the gentle breeze will not overturn me. If I gazed on naked reality, unclothed with beautiful lies, I'd be depressed, go mad."

"How sad. You cannot even recognize—"
"You ass, did you—"

"Don't commit the fallacy of *ad hominem* personal attack—"

"You asshole, did you think that this was a bloodless discussion with no consequences?" Coyote snapped, pulling out some flight feathers and a small piece of red flesh, "I can't improve my 'mythic fitness' by being only positive. I had to invent death so there would not exist only human beings and so that the continental islands would not sink under their weight. That was clever of me: I threw a stone into the stream; if it floated we would live forever, if it sank, everyone would die eventually. I had to lie to teach people the skills they needed to live: Caution, like I did with deer, lies and loss, and that things are never as they seem. I had to show them order and culture so that they could cope."

"So, lying is good and necessary?" Vulture asked as he jumped to a branch, glaring at a pulse in Coyote's throat.

"No, just entertaining. Hey, I see a mouse!" and Coyote raced away.

Coyote deconstructs his myth

Taking his lead from the learned Doctor Vulture,
Coyote decided to be educated. He put on a pair of glasses.
The Yellowjacket sisters seemed all abuzz
at his lecture at the 'Sneezing Lion Memorial Tree.'
Even owl was looking agog at Coyote's masterful presence.
Turtle and Mountain Lion were there too, but they both
seemed comatose or maybe just extremely contemplative.
  "The trickster archetype," he started, "exists in many cultures.
It is an old stereotype, older than the warrior, or king
or wonder woman. Indigenes—new word, heh—have many stories
of the trickster figure. This is so because we live in a dual
reality of opposite polarities, such as good and evil,
and Coyote only reflects that by exhibiting both tendencies.
The Trickster capital 'T' is a valuable and necessary
component of preter-human psychology. Without the trickster,
your little lives would dull and perhaps unbearable. Yet,
like everything else, the Trickster has a dark and a dark side,
I mean light side," and Coyote held out his foreleg and rotated
it so part was in shadow. "And that's the secret to that.
Light, dark, it's just shadow on the same substance. Nothing
to worry about folks. In this way we can give the trickster
a more positive or lighter note," and Coyote raised his forelegs.
  "Some Doctor Roangrim described the beloved Trickster
as a false shaman, a source of satire on the excesses
and abuses of shamanism. The heroic Coyote is clearly
an object of satire and ridicule for this reason. He is portrayed
as an incompetent charlatan who conjures phantoms that take
energy from the tribe and his careless, evil manner reverses
the traditional tribe-nurturing role of the shaman to serve
his own needs. Evil? This is a sad distortion of the truth. When
have I ever put my wants or momentary desires before your
needs?"   —One of the Yellowjacket sisters noted that
Coyote's penis seemed to be more alert—
  "Some Perfessor Shortgrizzle described Coyote as
a bricoleur, a mythic handy-man who cobbles reality in the form
of a bricolage out of the available material, which is quite
everything when you think about. It is also the first stage

of a mythic creative process, providing the botched magic
with which trickster unwittingly constructs the bricolage that will
determine the realities of the world to come. Coyote's so-called
blundering attempts at secrecy not only fail, they set a mythic
precedent—Coyote exposes everything, especially to females—
and if what he achieves is not what he intended, it nevertheless
represents a successful shamanistic endeavor. The false shaman,
in fact, becomes the mythic shaman. Impotence is transformed
into real power, absurdity into true meaning, and the trivial
into the consequential as Coyote the holy trickster
is unceremoniously—"

       "Which Coyote?" asked Bat, confused again.
"—shuffled from one role to another in a confusion of ironies
that is luminal, liminal, and subliminal, enlightening—"

    Coyote paused, trying to decide if he was praising himself
enough. "Stories of tricky Coyote are not meant to be taken
seriously. They are always educational. Often the stories
are funny, very funny, sometimes scatological, rarely
offensively overtly sexual—after all, they are for children."
Coyote paused and looked wise, his glasses sliding a little.

    "If a prostitute turns a trick, then Coyote is a Trickster.
Another trick, please. Quick," he said, smiling at Badger's
woman. "So, feed your inner Trickster, that is the lesson.
Do what you want. The symbolic trick has real ontological
significance when it acquires material existence," and
with that he defecated by the lectern.

Coyote changes Or one more trick sailor

Now, none of the women would have him, he thought,
but he knew that the men were, ah, less selective.
He had noticed some good-looking men, Bobcat and
Mountain Lion, for instance. There was even a new Coyote
on the edges of the territory. Coyote would do anything
for action. He sighed; maybe the professors were right.

Coyote took an elk's liver, warm and moist, and made
a vulva from it. Put it under his tail. Then he took two elk's
kidneys and made breasts from them. Put them on his chest.
Finally he put on a woman's dress. The Yellowjacket sisters
sewed him into the dress, enclosed him very firmly.
He stood transformed into a very pretty woman indeed,
not on close inspection though. He put a fresh mouse
in the sleeve. He was ready. The girls buzzed approval.

He walked down by the river, the liver chaffing his thighs.
but the dress swirled attractively. There beneath the pine
was the new coyote, as handsome as Coyote himself
and as full of himself. They talked, about the weather,
hot, and about the river, cool. Coyote waited for the other
handsome coyote to offer him—her now—a mouse.

He did. A plump mouse still alive, which Coyote gulped, then
remembered to say a sweet "Thank you." That male sure
was beautiful. Coyote was in love and ready to give
himself, if he could figure out how. He displayed his rear.
The other Coyote seemed awkward but it was over faster
than a human public road courting. They lay on the sand
under the shade, licking and snuffing and dozing.

Coyote was so pleased at the result that he flung
off his disguise and revealed his real masculine self.
The other young male gazed admiringly, then shed
his own mask—Coyota! His mate, mother of his pups!
This sucked! He had never been tricked, fooled, or so
recently humiliated. He threw his clothes in disgust

at the Yellowjacket sisters, who went in the sleeve
excitedly, and ate the mouse inside its fur.

Coyote started to stalk angrily into the river, but
Coyota grabbed his tail and pulled him back.
"You thought I was just a simple mother?"
she asked. "just good for a quick pump or cleaning up
the stuff from the pups? Huh?"

Coyote snapped around but missed.
She said, "I am just like you, a Coyote, and I like to play
the games of life and death, just like you, just like the mother
of all pups."

Coyote considered, "Why haven't I seen you before?"
"You have," she said, "but I was always a male when you saw
me, of course a graceful, clever male, flawless—"

"Okay, alright, I understand, but a female—
women cannot be tricksters. It is not right!"

"Why? why not?" she demanded.

"Mmfttthhh,"
Coyote raged incoherently, "because females are good
or perfect. It is not goodness that instructs. Not perfection
that screws up everything to drive development."

"Only a male would say that.
Females hate and plot as ruthlessly as any male.
You think that because you have your secret male
societies for hunting and gossiping that we do not?
We do. We can ruin a good thing as easily as you."

Coyote shook his head and headed towards
the hills, but Coyota nodded at the Yellowjacket
sisters, who stung him enthusiastically until he jumped
into the river.

Coyota caringly soothed her mate,
"I can get some good mud for those, and we can
talk. I had a good day. How was yours? I was
so attracted by that dress. Where did you get it?"
And they talked by the river, two tricky beings
delighting only in themselves for the moment.

Coyote overextends himself Or tricky dick in a fix

Coyote was watching Horse over on the mesa
eating tender shoots of bunch grass. Horse raised
his head locked his legs and his penis extended
almost to the ground and released water
in a stream. Coyote's eyes bulged.
'Have to get one of those' he thought, 'impress
the hell out of those new young foxes by the water
hole.' He ambled on up to Horse and said
"just noticed the length of your member—
could I borrow it?"

                     Horse snorted and said: "Ever
try to mount a mare? You need this just to get close
to the circle of—"

                  "I was thinking more for show,"
Coyote interrupted, "need to attract the attention
of someone."

               Horse chewed and pondered,
swallowed the green morsels and noted:
"Seen men, once, put a plant shaft over theirs.
See that boojum plant in bloom? Above the white sage?
Take the mast and slide it over your shaft. That
should get the girls liquid! Now, go away, before I kick you!"

     "Okay, okay." Coyote said, "I get the picture."
He slunk away, then out of sight pranced quickly
to the towering plant. He looked. He bit the spike,
then chewed and chewed it until it fell. Proudly
he surveyed his work. Getting it on, however,
was no mean feat. He had to lie on his side and use
his feet to slide the hollow tube over his limp
hollow tube, the splinters making it limper.
Not exciting he thought, but remembered the goal,
the plan, the purpose of the suffering.

Finally, he slipped it off, getting splinters
the other way, then stood, put it on,
then picked it up the middle in his teeth
and started towards the water hole. It was long

and awkward and knocked over a wasp's nest
and some flew in the end. They stung. He dropped it
on the ground for a rest. He got it up,
but his member had swelled from the stings
of the wasps. It was never coming off.
When he got it to the water hole, he peeked
over the grease bush and saw two girls
standing talking, tails high, waiting for a male
to pass by. After weeks of grunting and groaning
Coyote got it up. He moved forward but it plowed
in the sand and stopped him, Now too heavy to lift.
Coyote remembered the time, however briefly
that his fur had been bright blue, like bluebird's
and he remembered stealing the sun. Now he was just
a father, a husband, a bread winner and den digger,
no longer the idol of young females everywhere.
He would be again, if he could just move this
this pole thing. Simple physics. He levered it
up with another branch, but could not
move very fast. It looked like the girls were getting
ready to leave. He carefully picked it up in his teeth,
anchored by splinters on his penis. He trotted
towards the hole, then shouted, "Hey girls, look at
this!" but it fell from his mouth. Spirit, that hurt.
It bounced on the sand and pulled him down the slope
rolling, over and over. Splash!
                         The girls jumped in fear.
Conchita said, "What was that?" and Esmerelda answered,
"I don't know, but there isn't a female large enough—
the splinters alone—do you think he's alright?" she asked,
as they watched Coyote roll into the water, dragged down
by his pole. "Perhaps he thinks he's a swordfish. I don't
want to know."
                         "Oh, he worships the instrument
and not the juice, the lingam and—" Esmerelda giggled.
and they trotted back to the safe den of their parents.

From underwater, Coyote watched their tan and trembling
haunches recede from sight. He felt himself press

splinters—it was hard to breathe and he could not move
or get it off. He sighed and watched the bubbles rise,
then started to chew a hole in the side for air. Slowly
the small end of the plant raised above the surface.
Water gutted out, then sharp breathing sounds.
Gila woodpecker landed on the tip and started rapping
out his tune. Coyote groaned "get help" and started humming
in code, and woodpecker flew off straight to Gopher Tortoise,
whom he asked, "What can I do for this headache?"
Tortoise chewed meditatively and answered, "Stop using your
head and start heading your use. Give up beetles."

Coyote decided to pray. Shiva would know what to do,
being god of ecology and the young and the humble, like
Coyote himself. He might be away, though, in mysterious
India, directing traffic from an elephant or something wild.

     So Coyote thought he would pray to Hermes instead.
He knew he'd get action from Hermes, the god of one-night
stands, the patron of thieves, liars, and footloose
wanderers, and the guide for souls on their way
to the underworld, but Hermes didn't respond; perhaps
his nikes were wingless in those tight caves.

     Maybe Artemis, the keeper of the mysteries of death
as genesis of life, the lady of the beasts, would know,
could tell him what he should do. He could picture
her, now, babe of the beasts, skirt decorated with bees,
garlands of grapes above her breasts, strings of pale
bulls balls below them. He yearned for her, but she was in
the depths of her sanctuary, moaning about the damage he
Coyote had done to the sacred reputations of animals, gods,
girls, myths, and words.

Coyote conquers celebrity Bombay

Recovering from his last hard adventure, Coyote had
good times watching sports on television, at least
until Renren opened his big almost fully-grown
mouth and told Coyote that the average pay
for a shot was eight thousand dollars, hit or miss,
play or not. After that, it was hard to root for anyone—
even the underdogs made seven.

That's all they saw anymore, millionaires
playing ball, or millionaires pretending to be Cleopatra
or Joe Louis, or millionaires playing or telling us
how much people could help their businesses.

Millionaires at work, millionaires at war, millineries
at parties, millionaires at home, with children—only
people tolerated them because they wanted to become
them, at least Coyote did, and he hatched a plan.

Coyote knew he could become rich, but first
he needed a guide, someone who knew the ins
and outs, but first he had to piss like a Horse.
Coming back into the den, he saw the actress slash
socialite slash tramp, Bombay Chevrolet, daughter
of the famous auto tycoon (famous for not squandering
all of his massive inheritance). Coyote knew that he
could have her, if he could get to the human city
of New York, which name sounded to his ears
like the asthmatic bark of a dying ground squirrel.
He would set out immediately, after rubbing
noses with the kids and Coyota, and lying of course.

It took a while, even in this supersonic age, hitching
a ride on a sheep truck from Arizona to Virginia
then on a chicken truck from Harrisonburg
to Lewes Delaware. And from there, Coyote decided
to paddle a canoe to the island New York.
Coyote was paddling along the coast when

people called out from the shore: "Where you going?"
"Going to have the daughter of Donald Chevrolet"

"Only a moron would do that?" they said.
Coyote got mad, paddled in and turned them into chickens.
Then changed his mind and turned them into cows:
"You will be the cows meatheads need to eat."
He departed and went paddling. Pretty soon another
group of people asked: "Where you headed?"

He told them. They said: "Be careful. The balls
of other men are piled in front of her lodge."
Coyote appreciated this, so he came ashore and put
mussels and wild Atlantic salmon in the water by them,
then went on. At a place called Avalon he put ashore
and walked through the pine trees to a large hotel. Saw
a wrinkled old woman steaming blue crabs. He grabbed some.
"Coyote!" she smelled him, "what are you doing here?
why are you eating my crabs?"

Coyote looked at her
and said, "You know me?"

"Of course, you're famous. There
are books listing your legendary exploits with the peoples
of the continent."

"There are?" Coyote asked. "Can you see
me? The real me? As I am, as an immoral trickster idol?"

She said yes, she was sensitive and clairvoyant.
Coyote shook his head, this would not do,
she must be in tremendous pain. He chewed
on some pine gum, then spit in her eyes.
She became dumb and blind to the human comedy;
she was happy and thanked him. They talked about
where he was going. She warned him gently.
He told her who he was going to marry.
She said, "You be careful. She has a way
of making men go limp with mockery.
Take these pieces of rubber and when you are with
her, put them in your ears. Look into her body
but not in her mind or heart, which are black holes
without light or warmth." To thank Coyote for his gift

of comforting dullness she gave him also the masks
of a poodle, innocent girl, business consultant, and lawyer.
Coyote looked at them without understanding; they
were not like the masks of the wren, deer, goat, and bear
that he had used before. But, he could not refuse the gifts.
He put them in his kit, with the mask that Coyota had made
for him, a human mask with silver hair at the temples, to give
him dignity; she had called it the George Hamilton mask.

Finally Coyote reached the territory of the Chevrolets,
the Trumps, Buffets, and Duponts. He put on the actor mask
to make himself look older. And sat by the river. Nothing
happened. He walked up the island, through the artificial
canyons and then circled a large park at the center.
Shortly, it must be fate, the daughter, Bombay came by
with her friends Paris and Roma and saw him.
"He would make a good toy," she said, "let's take him back
to the condo and degrade him," which they did.
That night she asked Coyote to come to bed with her.
Coyote could hear the sound of mockery from under her
tortured hair. Once in bed he heard the sound of snickering.
so he put the rubbers in his ears and smiled at her,
reveling in her young, frequently-advertised body. She mocked
him, but frowned when it had no effect. Safe sex at last.
He took off his mask and showed that he was Coyote;
he had come to marry her. She agreed thinking it might be
a good career decision, and they tested the limits
of the bed, with screams and laughter.

When Donald Chevrolet heard laughter coming from
his daughter's room, he got up and came in. He said,
"Who is that with you, under the covers? Who's tail
is that?"
            She said: "that's my husband, welcome him."
      "Oh, please, spare me," said that Donald, and left.
The next morning Donald set a trap for Coyote, then knocked
on the door and requested Coyote to come out into
the cavernous breakfast nook to meet him.
Coyote put on the poodle mask and came out, to be caught

by one of the bodyguards, Steve, who tossed him over
the fortieth-story balcony.

Donald said, "Serves him right
for embarrassing me. Tell the doorman to clean up
the suicidal poodle's mess. And tell Bombie that 'fluffy'
couldn't stay." And he went out to an important business
meeting with his partners.   Far below, on the busy street,
Coyote took off the flat poodle mask and took the elevator
back to the penthouse, back to bed with Bombay.

The next night Donald heard laughing, so he just sighed
and set another trap. When Coyote came out with
the innocent girl's mask, one of the body guards, Reggie,
grabbed him and arranged for him to sold to an exotic
service industry outlet, where he was reamed day to
until dusk by foreign businessmen—before he was flat
and totally dry he took off the innocent's mask,
although he put it back on just long enough to get a cab
uptown. Bombay was having breakfast while her hair
was being trained. Coyote feasted on strawberries
the real authentic food of the gods; they went back to bed.

For the third time, Donald heard sounds of love-making
and laughter and again knocked on the door and asked
who was with his daughter, now. Bombay answered,
"My husband, you know that."

Donald shrugged in disgust
and gave orders for another trap. When Coyote came out
the next morning in the consultant mask, the bodyguard
Ivan paused, as Coyote said, "Think about your career,
I have more power than Donald and I could have you fried."
Ivan held up his open paws and stepped back. Coyote sat
down to eat with a surprised Donald,

"I thought
you were some damned musician or Greek sailor,
perhaps I was wrong."

Coyote took the financial pages
and occupied himself. Donald sat plotting a new plot.
"What are you doing with those figures?" Coyote asked.

"Those are stocks. I am making them grow."
"How do you do that? Is it easy? Could I do it?"
  "Maybe, here try. Punch in your numbers."

Finally, he asked Coyote to come with him and work on
a new business venture over on Wall Street. They took
the limo to his office. They invested in a venture that
Donald was sure would break Coyote. Coyote picked
up a stock certificate and chewed it quietly. Donald
asked Coyote to meet his obligations. When
the call came, Coyote was trapped by declining values.
He spat out certificates, and Donald thought Coyote
was through, hemorrhaging red ink. He said, "Serves
you right for trying to marry my daughter without
my permission," and left for the limo.

Coyote left the ruined consultant mask on the trading floor,
put on the lawyer's mask and raced out to the limo,
"Why did you leave me, dad, I was almost trapped?"
  "Oh, my fortunate son, so glad to see you, almost cried
myself to death when I realized that you had been ruined.
I thought, how was I going to tell my daughter? How did
you get out by the way? That's not possible."
They got into the limo and started home. Coyote was chewing
on a piece of shoe leather. When it was soft he carved
a policeman shape and threw it out the window, saying, "You
shall be the law." The law followed and grabbed Donald
as he got out of the limo.
                    "Get my lawyer!" Donald shouted.
  Coyote gave his card to the law and said, "I'm his lawyer.
I'll see my client tomorrow."
                    When Coyote got back
to the penthouse, Bombay asked where he father was.
Coyote said he didn't know for sure, probably the club.

Coyote makes his mark on Wall Street

Coyote signed the papers for the psychiatric assessment
of Donald and quietly assumed responsibility for running
the Chevrolet corporation. His first decision was to push
a car called the 'Coyote' to compete with the Cougar,
Mustang, and Viper. (Coyota heard. Furious that it was not
named after her, she stole a Miata for herself.)
With sixteen cylinders, it was so overpowered in the first
three gears that it caused numerous accidents and had
to be retired to the pantheon of Edsels and Thunderbirds.
Regardless of his inability to create a popular, efficient car,
Coyote ran the nonprofit foundation quite well, getting many
more animals, including Coyotes, protected by the EPA.
Furthermore, he was able, working with dirt first and other
human groups, to get Eastern Arizona made into a corporation
with a board of directors that included several snakes
(the original kind, thus decisive and responsible) so
the desert would be protected forever. He even
started a youth club called the Coyscouts of Arizona,
who were really good at survival training.

Bombay tired of him but could not dislodge him
from the penthouse or corporate offices. She screamed
that he was nothing but a cheap coyster bent on stealing
her family's fortune. He was bent though. Coyote had a short
affair with Roma but had forgotten to put rubbers in his ears—
she wanted her little coytoy, her ruffy-wuffy coybow,
to appreciate her voice and her lust for him—
he had forgotten how consuming the human tongue—
but by then he had a new mistress, power. Power.
He understood in his sly way that corporations had to please
their stockholders. His bodyguard Ivan counseled him
on entertainment and understanding of the lowest common
denominators of life, as if Coyote had never been so low.

Coyote knew what to do. He knew everything better
than anyone, so he never asked for no advice nohow.
He invested in a series of semi-domestic coyotes he called

'coyopets.' but they bit children and had to be recalled.
The series of transformer machines, called 'coybots,'
did marginally better, before they were recalled.
"I have to get richer," Coyote was saying to Crow,
"maybe something really cheap and simple—"
            Crow asked Coyote, "Why do you want to be richer?"
"For food, silly, and women, and finer furs, in richer colors.
Why do you birdbrains hide from wealth?"
        "I don't need to hide. Wealth avoids me. Poets can never
get rich selling their works, because everyone sees
themselves as poets, not being able to create pet rocks
or other technological accomplishments. No. A verse
is a gift; it cannot be otherwise, as it has no value, but it has
obligation, the obligation to reciprocate or to change."
Hmm, Coyote thought, and had Crow shown out the door.

The prices of houses sky-rocketed so people could not afford
them, and then the bubble collapsed. Countries called in debts
to forestall their fiscal slide. Conditions seemed bleak.
Coyote analyzed the downturns of the market and identified
some trends—after the civil war the public turned to circuses
for succor; after the depression, people lost themselves
in movies; after the bush league years, video games sucked
in the souls. Knowing that 2009 was going to hit bottom,
Coyote had the corporation sell off its cars to Kia
and invested exclusively in interactive holographic movies.
"Coyovision" took off—he was richer than Croesus or Gates.
Although horror themes proved irresistible, the remake
of a roadrunner cartoon—a different roadrunner
eaten each time, unable to escape from Coyote's clever
cars or rockets, unable to avoid capture—proved
to be uninteresting to kids or to mature consumers
so Coyote remained unknown and unworshiped
behind the new corporate logo 'Chevroplay.'
Then things changed in unexpected ways;
people no longer wanted to work to buy more things
at least beyond the 'Coyovision' wall unit.
Instead of rebuilding, instead of starting the up cycle
the economy stayed at the curved bottom.

Without being creative people tired of their toy.
Coyote had undermined the last dignities of civilization.
It was time to enron out. Leaving the deserted city,
he paused to piss on the corner of the building
at the corner of Wall Street.

Coyote trips, civilization falls

This was no fun, no fun at all. He went back to Arizona
because things were going to be really difficult now
and he needed to have a safe and secure place
to dwell in the colorful and comfortable desert.
From time to time, he ran into Fox and Bluejay,
who seemed to be traveling to a clean place also.

At a deserted gas station on 18, where the last sign
said nine dollars a gallon, he rolled in oil to get
the colors from light to reflect in his fur
for his triumphant homecoming to Coyota
but Coyota gagged and made him bathe.
She said the pups had grown and moved to Seattle
and she Coyota was ready for more.
Coyote knew he was in trouble
when he saw she was wearing the mask
of the handsome male, the mirror
coyote that Coyote loved.

Meanwhile people became less interested in working
and making things they did not need, more interested
in talking to other people, and enjoying life,
and so things fell apart. So what,
thought Coyote, just another cycle down.
Many people left the cities; some stayed and started
growing food on rooftops. People flooded to farms
and overused the land and left, but a few stayed
and started permacultures. Some fled
to the forests and deserts, but could not make

the land provide, after killing off antelope
and even eating rattlesnakes fried in oil.

Rattlesnake asked Vulture, "What—"
and that was all the good Doctor needed:
"—is the moral of all this, that Coyote has done?
You ask, you were asking that of course.
There is no moral, none, nothing,
no meaning, no tragedy. Things just happen
that might have happened anyway. Good causes evil,
evil causes good, then all that fervor decays
into the fertile soil for more life, which goes on,
sometimes questioning itself
sometimes not—"
                        "But Coyote, he made things worse."
"Oh, for you maybe, but not in the long run;
he just mixed things up, added to the soil. Well,
he shit on everything and shit is good, it fertilizes
soil—"
            And Rattlesnake coiled and started rattling,
so Doctor Vulture lifted lopsidedly above the Palo Verde
above its exquisite blue blossoms and said:
"I know, your sorrow is not lessened or diminished;
it is real and painful and you can follow the chain
of events from Coyote to the death of your young.
Why not just bite Coyote and feel better—
who knows, things might get better now."
and Vulture circled up, spiraled way above
the desert floor on a column of rising air.

The next valley away, Coyote lay
flat, dusty and unmoving—
(The end? Oh, sure, yea, you wish!)

senseless

carbon dreams
what we dream as elements is to match our charges
with the others and form bonds that keep us close
and stable through the chaos of emotion.
the angle activates the form   as elements weave
through bodies make connections partnerships
an even number or a stable form.
carbon subverts the angel of dreams by changing
electron charges. by its evenness the images
become static perfect platonic forms without interest
or depth.

machine dreams
digital randomizations with narrative connections
from experiences—daphne from the tree,
dolphine as metamorphosis slow changes, like aging only slower,
over more than one lifetime, with machines overlapping
like mechanical metaphors.
irreverence is the modern attitude
and has the certainty of machines, based on the neutral
values of mechanical science.
rock is the base geological thingness.
words are nothing compared to holocausts in europe,
or asia, or africa, or any unknown place or species.
words are leaves next to the inventions of technology,
the weak imitation of hardness.
what can follow science? knowledge plus value plus ethics,
as a way of living? way? daring exploration tempered
with caution and understanding but done peacefully
without harm to our natural matrix? nature, the word, the idea,
is abstracted from the ground of existence.
machine city is a wasteland of abandoned—
a warehouse of unused constructs. with vision we make order
to change chaos but vision illuminates the chaos clearly
and 'the wild sky sings'

school trap

what did school teach me?
that those who are better schooled are superior.
that those who have more money will have a separate
schooling that will keep them separate and elite.
that knowledge is power and power is a trap
and if you understand then you can live in it and be happy?
i did not learn well enough.

academic poultry

time passed indubitably while i wrote exponentially
scribble scribble, scribble, eh, mister dullun
for my entire reputation not to mention my violet tenure
rested on my ability to impress the wearers of academic dress.
the psychoanalysis of mutant values consumed my life—
is barbarism compatible with deformed configuration?
is speech expressive of the capture of my singularity? Yes!
it is the vehicle of flesh and the sculpture of love
semiotic fluxes and machine phyla are indisputable
proof of mechanical life polarity is bound to vanish.
the spector of housework haunts my words with dishes,
laundry, and dirt a problem with the distribution of labor
and my own political power who has to harness
the machines to liberate my time from—

i saw the poultry in harness to the cold didactic muse preparing
her texts for the vortex of war— i knew i had no excuse
and had to call incisive flames and release the ghosts of meter
but, the poultry was hopping, jumping from seed to seed
of every idea or justification to continue living wild
and i could not focus my weapons of mass destruction
i destroyed place after place but the body count did not increase
according to projections.
                                            recenter the ecology of human greed.
through the rear-view mirror darkly to the light satanic mill
and factory went immaterial transformation on the backs
of mechanical dogs of war from clay-mation

to glassine vaults light brutalism triumphant! what is celebrated?
heroic dildos? or urban gothic swizzle sticks in plastic sleeves?
what is the target? feminine purity?
the round is ready, pull the trigger! penetrated by the metal
gift the body transcripts the message. the mission is over,
rest easy. eject the shell.
Protoplasm ripens long before the consciousness
then consciousness bifurcates and i can see above
and below the cloud standing on the heads of scholars.
i think i never should have left the house without my rubbers,
of course. my feet were wet; it was just a dream so i reached
for the pen and thesaurus to deconstruct and to transcribe
the essence of its metaphysical meaning and liberate the future.
modern poultry is the attempt to overcome silence,
expounded professor pisser silence is the shape of failure,
he declared but only silence answered him that is,
silence as the bearing field of poultry, the proper attitude
of the living body, loud in its insistence.
when life is perverted by interference, extinctions,
holocausts, then silence can be left behind to invent
a better reality or rather return to silence
gracefully, gratefully, mindfully fully.
the universe of truth and beauty is chasmic
from the heterogenous ontology of lust, because the rupture
is subjective and only the leaping genius of men can fuse —
only art can capture the trivial forms of stature and inform
the shape of rapture to guide the path of speech to exceed
the curse of limit— oh, miasma, chaosmic spasms plague
our little horizons. oh, the sadness, the waste
the car-wrecked generation of writers, the boozy artists
of cool provocation and woe sitting in their hummers
writing what they know rapping what they dream.

roll me

never forgot a face that paid a dime to roll me
never forgot the dollar that rocked me
or the ten to rock and roll on the sleeping bag
over plastic bags, sliding in mockery.
not forgetting is a curse.
it is only touch i want, the faceless gentle wrapping
rapture, the backrub or caress not the fuck
and the strained talk
i never remember the touch and forgetting
that is more than i can bear
but there is always someone i can pay or trade
for time and if i cry
i can always say it is with indescribable pleasure

bonfire of creation

into the bonfire went his paintings
freed from the flaws of human expression
and the limits of simple skills. the flaws disappeared
never to be seen or remembered
he watched them move to dreamtime by degrees,
by particles, the ideas now immortal, waiting only
another instance of form in paint or gesso
too many symbols to outline a simple idea,
too many arguments for a basic philosophy
that and its waste, paper

Paion (wherein the author calendars a charm for complexing
comrades while cranes climb clouds with pedigrees)

Land is laid
The ocean is done
and I have only just arrived.

The first step is ambiguous
the second becomes ambition
and the third destination

Vestiges trace the verse.
Alternate footprints pave the halo
in miniature on colonized ground.

Weeds and their ideas grow larger
without lines.
The seeds are spread in wisps
that blind the window and profit weeds.

The secret is not in the helix
nor in the flesh
but the living curved expression.

We fashioned a pyramid
with ourselves at the top
but we are only hybrids of ideas.

Angels without enthusiasm are like bees
without mellilotus
        not free but lost barren imaginings.

The brown heart of the bear consents
to a bonfire of boughs
and branches.

Astonished by green flame
the lynx is calm and watchful
in the twilight.

Raven is noisy,
no raven is noise airsick
and uncertain.

infant insults a mouse idiot sharks an idea
Squirrel monsters disorder—
None speak.

Struggling to speak to be heard
amidst the agony of many,
we open.

Wine has its other uses
in the symposium
of life than to fill skeletons.

Lying in grass imbricating,
accosting each other,
learning stillness and silence.

Faust Reconsiders

Faust: "Where is the mind that conceived a world,
bore it and cherished it, joyously
released it to the air and inflated it to rival
our very spirits?"

Gadai: "The wind rustles brown leaves
in the fall, but it isn't the wind that ends
the lives of leaves, or takes the green
somewhere. it is another fuse
that we only feel but cannot see."

Faust: "With greedy hands you dig for treasure,
and are happy when you find earthworms!"

Gadai: "Exactly! The hands are in the earth
helping ideas to give birth."

Faust: "To what? To art, that is so long!?
Or to life, that is so frivolous and short?"

Gadai: "To chaos, wild chaos! The joy of destruction,
the loss of the weight of having, of memory,
lets us bloom in chaos, then be sucked
back to bloom elsewhere.
Christ, how many others have there been,
who loved woman or man, and left them for a promise?
Was it happiness to go?

Faust: "You'll soon get bored with fields
and forests. Never envy any bird his flight."

Gadai: "Spirit's pleasure bears us both,
from volume to volume, and those
are only symbols of life."

Faust: "I am the spirit that always denies!
A good thing, isn't it, for all that exists
deserves to be destroyed. it would have been
so much better if nothing had been created."

Gadai: "I am the spirit always denied
and I have not even lived, being obligated
to ideas and the requirements of life
and nothing, no one, has ever made me sated."

Faust: "It is so hard to contain two urges
at once, to be and to not be,
or to love nature and to master nature.
I have done it."

Gadai: "I can not, I will not. And now time
has moved on, and free of fear
and awe we choose mastery
and nonbeing. Difference is unimportant
to people today, ignorant of the loss."

Still Life: The Artist's Dirty Clothes

Black and white stripped shirt, one arm
over brown corduroy jeans. Black and green chevrons
on a gold velour pullover, tangled
grey trousers. Blue sheets under the pile.
A chef's coat stained with red paints like a surgeon's
smock covered with blood—it was a critical operation
brown socks, blue sock holding
     empty positions white turtleneck
by the pine dresser; blue shirt folded on a green carpet
The costumes and masks laid aside
     Moods attach themselves to clothes
and color their wear, after the fabric fades from washing
who recounts the history of clothing,
or the collapse of forms, follows
the dialectic of thread? Only the washer.

Swimming at Night

Swimming out into the gulf, being lifted and dropped
by waves, slowly then looking back, amazed
at how distant the shore has become—
have I demanded enough, too much from myself?
is there more that I can become, by exertion
or extension? I know the land is beneath me under
the water so what catastrophe can happen?
it is not water I fear but darkness
and if I pray often enough for light then my life
will always be like the inside of a pearl
or wave in front of a ray.

The Secret of Life (Version 1283.7)

Nothingness in quantity converts itself to being to thingness
Stillness in quantity converts itself
To motion
Quantity to quality sameness to difference completeness
to awareness oneness to otherness— Is this the secret
of god bored with oneness and completeness desiring
to be more, and, less?
Is this the secret of cancer to be immortal like god to convert
everything to itself and die? and be spread out? To return
to completeness and quantity stillness and nothingness?
The game is converting, conversing
Everything converts itself into something else
Something that can be the ground that cannot support itself
anymore much less the lightest thought or theory
and conversion is a trap, once converted it cannot
go back but you can remember and converse about it.

No, it can convert, and does.
it reverts to its previous state
but the pattern moves on
and the pattern can move without the matter
in its form in its particularity
like a blue guitar or palm tree in the mind

Hydrogen converts itself to helium, iron
to actinium, single elements to molecules,
molecules to enzymes,
and only great force can revert them.

Enzymes to organs
accidents to reproduction, single cells to many,
single levels to embedded levels, planes to folds
and lines to active coils, and it continues,
duplication to sex.

And hydrogen converts its home, reducing to oxidizing,
sea to land, land to air, fins to hands,
cartilage to spines, jelly to skin,

skin to carapace or feathers
spewing and spawning to internal eggs
carriages to cars, coal to fusion,
finger counting to computers

People convert forests to grasslands, and grasslands
to fields of wheat and those to dust, and dust
to concrete and lung disease. The final conversion
is not always what we intended.
Weeds convert bare ground into a paradise
of weeds, but the work of weeds,
the shade of weeds, the mold
and litter of weeds
provides the homes for flowers and trees
that crowd out weeds
who have to bank their seeds
and wait for the next conversion back to bare ground.

Rock is converted to pyramids, people are converted
to pyramids of power and value, animals and algae
to parts of the pyramids. The pyramids become inverted
and animals become more valuable, and weeds and bacteria
become most valuable. What is value but what is wanted?
Dung is more valuable than gold to a beetle
who converts it to the flesh of beetles.
Converted, reverted, perverted, change moves
through traps remaking the traps from the flesh
of the trapped. And value inverts so what is needed
is desired more than what is rare, but you know that.

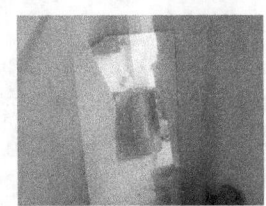

homeless

these guest writings were shared by my friend babe martin,
called by many at her own urging, 'psychobabe,' and they
chronicle her descent into homelessness. she was not only
a woman, not only once a respected doctor, but a certified,
accomplished, deeply-convicted crank allowed on the streets
only due to gross judicial incompetence. she started writing
an advice column in the globe, but after a while it appeared
dribbled in motor oil in back of Porter's store. despite
setbacks in her native boston, she continued to write the advice
column, but now it appeared scratched on hundreds of unreadable
notes kept in her sixteen plastic shopping bags, at her new home
boston alley 56 off marlborough street (she was used to the best
after all).

stages of defeat

you keep working, but are dominated by your tragedy;
you lose interest in eating or sleeping. you clean your home,
though, still thinking about the event, and rehearsing
your reactions over and over and over.

you sleep with the aid of pills. you eat quite a bit, but only
good, sweet foods, because this is the only good thing
in your life at this time. you go to work but leave early
for appointments. mid-day amusements, such as bowling
or drinking, rank high.

you are annoyed by the good attentions (or neglect)
of your friends and family. you cannot be reached. you sleep
much more; work becomes an unpleasant memory. alcohol
or other chemical modifiers retain their fascination.

useless things, such as furniture, coin collections, leather
shoes, or appliances, seem to trickle away from you, like
urine down a sidewalk. you get angry when your musings
get interrupted. you retreat to your cardboard-covered
piece of sidewalk.

you are amused by the preoccupations of others,
the time-driven, money-oriented, thing-obsessed many.
you notice birds, rodents, flowers, and weeds. you get
more exercise and have a more balanced diet,
depending on the dumpster route. you are free.

life goes on, does it?

"waddaya wan?" she asked.

                     "my friends they told me life
must go on," he said.

                "oh, a patient," she pursed her lips
and nodded, "have a seat over here, on this can. my fee
is twenty-five cents, or a bottle," she stared at the brick
wall, forgetting the bottle for a moment, her voice, now,
as soothing as any medicine: "they said life must go on?
why? where's it going? tell me your story, the whole thing,
chronologically."

he did, while she poked at a pile of rags with a stick.
"you lost everything," she agreed, "your wife, your home,
children, investments, retirement, car, job—your clothes
are nice, you still have those." he fingered his sleeve.
"you could start over, going back to school or getting
a new job, save for another twenty-five years, buy new
things, find a woman, start a family—but there is no rule
that it all cannot be taken away again. if i were you, i'd go
for society's throat, start selling guns to children, try
writing crucial messages on walls, drop out of the system,
off the grid, subvert people with radical ideas, move
to cambridge. "life goes on, things get better, life
is good—ha! myths, just myths to enslave you. you could
stop, just do nothing, not work or eat—protest, make
a statement, or stay here with me, i could teach you—"

mean of life

ed, a young bearded homeless man in camouflage
clothing and sneakers asked, "is this it? this is it? everything?
where is there any meaning?"

"do you expect meaning?"
she answered, straightening the newspapers over her sore-
covered legs, finding a crumb of godiva chocolate
(she was used to the best after all) on page seven.

"yes, i do," he said, "otherwise why bother?"
"why bother what?" she replied, "living? eating, sleeping?
have you seen the alternative? a plastic box in pile of dirt
near a church?" she reached and moved a greasy lock
of hair from his nose. "listen, you don't have to be here,
you could go house to house asking for work, others
have gotten lucky, it just takes one break." she poked
one of her less certain molars and continued, "the meaning
here is simple, through a combination of bad choice, bad
luck, bad economics, and a society that cherishes selfish
entertainment, you have been sorted from the comforts
of rewards to the light disposal area tolerated on the fringes.
there is plenty here, it's not like india for christsakes,
look at your sleeping bag—it's waterproof. your nikes,
your whatever—

"you know for months i slept in the cab of a rusty reo truck
until it was taken over by railhead red—did i complain?
no, because it is not the fitter who survive but the most
cooperative. life is not won by people with the most money,
but enjoyed by those who are most open to the freshness
of an october leaf, like this one," she traced its veins
under a scarlet blaze. "this doesn't mean anything, it just is.
we just are, everything just is and continues until it does not.
never mind, i sound like a soundbite for death.
could you get me a drink of water, please?"

f-art

espied i it on my way to the university dumpsters.
it hunkered into the pavement by the student union,
as if embarrassed by its own lack of symmetry or meaning,
a misshapen blob of metal and dirt, unrelated
to its surroundings, disconnected from any theoretical
or autistic i mean artistic foundation. there are those
who criticize this kind of art, saying that the artist
exercised no vision and little discipline, other than signing
it and pocketing the fee. not only will i defend such art,
but i urge the expansion of the category to include
my own contribution to art, 'found art,' f-art in short.
for example, later that same day, i saw a perfect example
of an organic torroidal concretion left on the sidewalk,
unique in its textural composition, and forceful in its
ontological presence. delicate in its compositional
harmony. discrete in its colors— so many shades
of brown and grey— engagingly multidimensional,
it was a veritable metaphor of the complexity
and brevity of life, a celebration of the joy of eating
and excreting. it was shit. true, shit. but art is
coprophilous as well as abstractly symbolic. and this
expression was as evocative as the pile of metal and dirt
seen in the morning. can we not all recognize the art
in everything, and respect it? careful, though,
not to step in it?

ravenna freedom

   "i don' understand. the streets aren't freedom?" Phil asked.
"it used to be," she said, "that being disconnected, from organizations,
companies, or churches, meant freedom. now it means
having no money, no home, nothing anyone wants. oh, yes,
i am still free, but freedom has lost a lot of meaning.
i would prefer to be free to have a garden, to build
something a little better than this cardboard, tin
and carpet coat castle that you see.

"that was what wilderness used to mean you know.
it was the symbol for freedom. you could be free
in the forest, free to hunt, and explore. now, i am here
in seattle and i am free to walk from second street
south and then under the freeway and up the hill,
as long as i come back, and am not discovered
underneath the ravenna bridge, oh merde.

"the system shall eat you up and spit you out,
then blame you for being eaten and excoriated
into a little piece of crap wrapped in someone
else's throwaway clothes."
        "you survive."

"i am not surviving. oh, the first time i lost
my job at the hospital—i was a doctor
you know—i laughed about it. the triumph
of petty bureaucrats over the independent
thinker concerned with granting a good
death to people in indescribable pain. then
later, i lost my job as grade school nurse.
that was a death sentence. i had nowhere
to go. after a time, money flowed away
and suddenly i had no place, no friends
who could give me another night on
the couch; no cash, no handouts. i became what
you see now. my fall was more dramatic than most,
but i understood what was happening better
than most. and, now i cope better than most but
i remember locked doors and sleeping through
whole nights, i remember ..."
                "hey, wanna get warm?"

xxx-mas

"this is it? this is it? the gift of the seasons?"
she hurled the old sock away.
"no, thank you, i have everything that i was given at the start,
eyes to see, lungs to breathe, all the equipment
to live and meditate. this crap that people
have to have, it is that, crap,
and that is what is pornographic,
not people intersecting their various curves in photographs,
but the lust to have more things than
you can carry, more than you can even see at once,
more than you ever need,
more than you have time to appreciate or care—
you know, time is the greatest gift to be given,
and that is all you really have to give that is your own.
and that is all i want, just some more time,
to lie under the cedar in the rain ...
ahh, to rest ... and see ..."

alley angels

"have you ever seen angels?" he asked.
          "you mean fat bald white men with 900-dollar shoes
handing out twenty dollar bills? yes, once," she sighed.
          "no, i mean beautiful romance book hunks and babes
comforting the sick so they don't go postal and make
more people miserable—well, maybe fat black women blessed
with the wisdom of poverty, well, you know what i mean."
          "no, no, i prefer quakers to angels. they can feel."
     "would you like to see, feel an angel?"
          "feel an angel's soft breath, fetid with methane like
any hungry cow. no. why?"
                    "but they are real, we must praise them!"
"sure, yeh, hail divas of earth and sky, pour your healing fluid
on our poor lives, come to our aid and guard our meager
lives and be with the blessed children and elders."
          "amen, woman."
                         "but can they give us soup"
     "are you bitter?"

"don't know, never ate my own flesh,
not that desperate yet"
    "are you sour?"
                "get off my coat, and be glad that we are free
to breathe and fly like any startled pigeon."

origins

"stop looking at me! just take a picture and eat it. well?"
        "i know you"
"not in a biblical sense i hope"
                            "no, from the library. i looked
you up on the internet"
                        "it may have been a mistake to show
you the library— libraries are for sleeping, not for tracing."
        "i couldn't help it, you are fascinating."
    "only in abstraction. i shit my pants this morning."
        "as normal as breathing."
                            "will you clean it up for me?"
"if you can't."
                "never mind. what travesty did the internet
show, what did you find?"
                            "you were a doctor, you helped
people achieve a good death."
                            "you understand?"
"you kevorkianized them."
                        "you don't understand."
"you gave them a choice, the power to choose, the strength
to choose."
        "you do understand, maybe. now what?"
    "tell me why?"
                "are you one of us?"
                                "us?"
"the really homeless or are you a reporter? one of them?"
    "them?"
            "the entertainment predators? the users?"
he fingered his beard, combing it with his nails: "no, just
a seeker of knowledge."
                    "knowledge or curiosities?"

"things, facts, science, myths, stories ..."

"everything, everyone
has a story," she smiled, probing a weak tooth.

"i know," he said, "and it would take a lifetime to tell it,"
he pontificated.

"don't be silly," she said, "most of life is habit
and repetition. no biography should be over a hundred
pages long. it simply isn't interesting to hear about
the thousandth clinical fuck or millionth beery binge"

"or the tenth patient?"

"or the second patient, dammit. people
want, need a private death, like any road kill cat."

"how did you get here?"

"i offended the medical
profession. i took my oath too seriously, have you ever read
that oath?"

"no."

"read it first."

"tell me first."

"pledge, help, no harm ... of course so much is unsaid
and left to interpretation. it should be rewritten for modern
body mechanics." she pulled at her underwear:
"we should discuss this later, after our ablutions."

"can sweet words make messy functions sound elegant?"

"fuck off and get me a newspaper."

"here," he pulled one
from his bed, "would you tell me how you got here?"

"thanks," she tore off a piece of paper and wiped inside
her pants. he watched without commenting, but scratched
his neck, thinking a flea, another carnivore.
"here in sarasota," she started, "it's so much warmer than
on marlborough street, and i do believe i've found
the fountain of aging, or at least it would seem so to those
who do not drink from it. you're too young
to be homeless."

"there are many younger."

"but, unless you like it, the young can always get jobs or
sponsors."

"you mean pimps?"

                              "no, sometimes just people
who help."
            "you mean angels."
                              "don't test me. why are you
here?"
      "i offended the legal profession."
                                    "is that possible?"
she gasped dramatically, "what, you denigrated forty
percent fees?"
                  "no, an ignorant judge, who let a ward
of the court suffer, i, well, i … i left under bad circumstances,
owing time and money to that same court."
      "good for you, dear, now let's try the dumpster on
fourteenth, i'm sure the story can wait."
                              he smiled and shrugged;
it wasn't going to be as easy as he'd thought.
      she thought that if she ever read anything about
herself in that yellow paper, this guy was going
to have to be sent to sleep with the manatees.

tao of home
"welcome home, babe!"
                        "home, what home?"
                                    "sorry. what's this?"
"sleeping bag, not a home not a place."
            "what about those people, us?" he asked, gesturing.
"we homeless are becoming so many and so many more
are becoming homeless not because we cannot find or keep
our homes but because the homes are being destroyed
the whole mother f-ing frame for homes is falling apart
not just for people but for mammals and frogs and other
beings. not bacteria though or viruses or molds or rats
or cockroaches—we are making more homes for
them each time we try to destroy them with chemicals
and poisons, medicines and cures, we offer them more
opportunities, more places for them and strengthen
their holds on those places but we could not live

in those homes."

      "so?" larry asked, "they live with us."
"so i guess we are making more homes with a net gain
and that is very taoistic that the lowest shall flourish
and the largest and richest shall fail and disappear.
poetic justice is better than no justice at all. at least
there shall be a universe of bacteria, amoeba and cells
if wolves, frogs, and humans cannot make it."

      "ouch, scrolled ideas way too heavy for a soggy
cardboard universe."

the use of children

"you have children?" ted asked, picking his nose
and flicking the prize onto the sidewalk.

      "is there a reason you're asking, professional
or personal?" babe asked.

      "jesus, you're suspicious," ted stood
up. she nodded. ted continued, "alright, i was thinking of
my daughter. hadn't heard from her in a while."

      "why wouldn't you live with her?"
"she's useless."

      "all children are useless, we push them out and force
them to behave our way. then our children push us out
and away, and we pull them out and in. then they antidote
our doting on the tired environment by burning it. and we
all warm ourselves by the flames and plant seeds in the ashes."

      "what? but i worry about her."
"and i worry about him. i tried to get him to lighten his load."

      "who? who is him?"
"never mind, you never met him. i put his paintings into
the bonfire, freed them from the flaws of media expression
and limits of simple skills. the flaws disappeared never
to be seen or remembered; i watched them move
to dreamtime by degrees, by particles the ideas now
immortal, waiting only another instance of form in paint
or gesso."

      "what a waste," ted said, spitting over to the gutter,

"whose child are you?"

"doesn't matter, hold me,"

"hold me, roll me, kiss ..."

"shut up," she said, leaning over.

the herd heads south
like that movie, urban cowboy, the sick and tired moved
south by bus to a new world of play and warmth.
and a new beginning. why did i go? she thought, i'm dying
of cancer as my body is subverted by immortal cells
that do not concern themselves with the welfare
of their host, a benign disease that does not offend
with pustules or flying mucus, just the slow decay of bones
as tumors replace the bone. i cannot fall again, that is all.
i cannot get sick, and cannot host a cold.

her first visit was to a grocery store. a new chain to her,
called publix, pubics she called it, but built on the same
model of a fluorescent heaven, displaying the cornucopia
of food and drugs. she was able to sample many
of the foods discretely. it was made easier by the fact
that some old people were stationed at tables by the end
of every aisle giving out samples of pizza, fish, and crackers.

she was speaking to her neighbor, 'tommy flash,' "had trouble
crossing the street, these drivers they do not care
and do not look unless they take aim."

"next time, take an empty grocery cart with you;
the drivers cannot risk damage to their hummers or toyotas."

"good idea, then i can turn it over and sleep under it."
"do you have a place? no? it is summer now, so the getting
is good. why, you ask? the snow-bird bums have moved north
for richer panhandling circuits. here, let me show
you a good place. 'soldier bob' left last month. he was living
behind those condos, by the fence. you can only be seen
from a small path there by the stream, oh, or by an alert
shopper at bealls, but they rarely look that far. oh,

and you will need a spot to sit. soldier bob used to sit
by the exit near the publix, but it was hard for cars to stop
there. i'd suggest that curve by the pond—people can see
you in advance and pull out of traffic to hand you a dollar.
you have an advantage, being a woman and all; there are few
of you and you get more concern, if you play it.
me? no problem. i have my places further down the tamiami
trail, near the college. students are well off and generous,
when being homeless is thought to be a romantic
career move."

the herd rests

she took his advice. nevertheless she was surprised when
he visited her a week later, with a proposal. "let's take a trip
to dizzeyworld with animal ed. he's got a car for the day.
it's only a two-hour drive to dizneyworld."
      she sputtered: "dizneyworld? epcot center?"
"hey, i never heard of apricot, what is that?"
      "never mind. how do we get in?"
"tickets, left over from graduation; i got six. you know
anyone else wants to go?"
      she shook her head, at a loss for words.
the ride was at high speed, although not as fast as the south-
bound bus had been. she watched the landscape flow by,
wondering what would it be like to run this fast? a new
race of people who needed speed and could not bear
to move slowly or to give slow things their attention.
at the edge of the parking lot she paused. her friends
stopped too, but looked into the gates, eager to taste
the treats. she started walking again, more slowly, letting
herself be dragged by the guys. all she remembered
of that day was lines, punctuated by brief action rides,
then more lines before food. of course, they also checked
out the trash cans, even found a ten-dollar bill wedged
against a fence. she decided to find a place to rest.
when she was sitting in the shade a coyote stopped in front
of her. she spoke to him, recognizing the trickster inside—

no normal coyote would be so calm and composed
in human crowds. he was a handsome brown, except
for a spot of mange near the tail. she invited him to stay
in the shade with her, but said that the blanket was clean
and hers. she looked into his eyes, sure that she had
offended him with her prim possession of the blanket,
but the look in his eyes faded suddenly and he burped,
sending a toxic scent of gases her direction.
she could smell old hot dogs and popcorn. she automatically
said," take some ginger for that, or else baking soda."
the look of intelligence and mischief returned to his eyes;

      Coyote thought perhaps she might be a colleague of doctor
vulture, but she was not made-up, groomed or dressed
for professional success; he smelled urine and her body
odors. he licked some grass from her knee, then trotted
out into the crowds, looking for his family.

      she lay down on her blanket and waited for the men
to return from their trip to the rest room to take showers.
then she could get cleaned up.

death in a teacup

later that same memorable day she saw the face of death
riding in a teacup, with a strange smile. she waited for him
until the ride had ended and spoke, "how can i see you?
are you real? am i getting ready to die?"

      —surprised, he answered, "you have been acquainted
with death before. i am just the face of the process,
makes it easier."

         she spread her hands but said nothing.
he said, "in time, but your bones have reached a plateau
that could extend for years. just keep your immune system
healthy. more fruits and vegetables, vitamins, extracts,
and enzymes. you'll be fine." he touched her hand.

      she was not able to se his eyes very well.
she asked him more questions and he answered them.
she asked questions about her friends, about life and death,
and meaning—

        it was so hard to remember meaning when

all there was around you was sun, money, palms, and fun.
every uncertainty and unpleasantness pushed out
of sight and beyond the edge of consciousness,
so this seemed like normalcy, waiting for rides, eating,
anticipating another day of hurrying and resting.
she could not wait to get back to her palm by the fence
and contemplate everything. she had expected to see
giant mice and fat pleasant burghers enjoying them,
not a mythical trickster or the face of death. she ran
her fingers through her hair, traced her breasts, rubbed
her thighs, relishing the feeling of being alive,
homeless, but free.

three shadows

I looked at my face in a glass and saw doubt in the shadow
of my eyes like the prey sees greed in the shadow
of the glutton's heart. I looked at my fingers
in the shadow of a cloud as short light sees the cancer
in the shadow of my bones—mad growth without limit
or shape or contribution to the whole pattern—
just a selfish thrust of life without limit or community.
Lucent lesions burning lesions from the gentle kiss of light
and a few small toxins absorbed with water.
Lucent darkness, lucent shadows from wild light,
three shadows connected only by wild dark,
mad words, poor images in the distance.
Long after water has gone, the river bed remains
then shadow becomes denser
energy folds its wings and dives
into dark, mocking light and grief, still light
light damage and now still life.
The next loaf of bread should be a life-time supply.
Pain is a strange thing; its absence gives pleasure
that is purer than any mere addition of sweetness. the ants
have gone away, but they will return. the sun feels good
and death is just one more night ...

lifeless

every story ends in death
you held his head while he vomited
thinking it could only get better
but knowing that you could never
see that white woolen carpet again
without the ghostly yellow stain.

> you rubbed her head until she slept
> looking up at the textured off-white
> ceiling as your future together unfolded
> as a series of happy vignettes where
> each success was surpassed by another.

you nursed him after the crash then through
the cancer treatments and finally
after the stroke that took his soul's identity.
now, nothing is left but the tenacity
of life sticking to the beating heart.

> after making love sublimely, she said:
> "i'm too fat, too old (29), my skin
> is loose," and she pushed her ears back
> and looked in the mirror and nodded.
> and you could see the future stretch
> out, repetitively, but you love her.

you each vowed that you would stay together,
in love, regardless of flaws and errors of judgment,
regardless of fate and all the permutations of time
thrown in your way, and you almost made it—

but every story ends in death, in bed on soft grey
and yellow striped sheets or on the concrete
illuminated by a few hard lights, under stranger's
gazes, who think that their story will be different.

logger dies, forest lives

he cut his foot off with his ax
screaming, then lying still
he saw the sky between the trees
for the first time, blue

the blade is balanced now
as it was not in its descent
the past all pointed—from buying the land
to the choice of boots— to this accident
he noticed a cedar frond by his arm
the pain was bearable the day complex
his sobs and cries not heard he stopped
and listened the blue jays stopped calling
the tree stood still the ground absorbed
his blood a thousand lives were fed.

seeking good death

joe got off work and came home careful
to take off the greasy coveralls with his name stitched
on the pocket. he relaxed in his favorite chair
and when pearl came to get him for dinner
she could not waken him from sleep.

bette lost her grip on the cliff edge
falling is easy, she thought then looked at
the clouds above her until they disappeared.

paul reached for the slab of wood then knew
he shouldn't have, his hand was gone
before he could shout to stop the saw.
after the blood slowed, he composed himself.

darlene slipped as she crossed the stream
fell and hit her head. the current took her corpse
then played with it, lifting the arm, turning
the head, before depositing it onto sand to rest.

cycling down the mountain, alan saw the crack
before it launched him into the rocks—
he bounced and bounced until he successfully
rolled to the canyon floor.

the grizzly crushed jim's skull, sniffed
the remains and ambled away.
small worms explored still passages
until the tunnels collapsed.

when ann stopped swimming, she sank;
the arms floated to embrace,
then fish distributed the gift
among the levels of the sea.

hannah lay in the grass, watching flowers
until no breath disturbed their petals.

death writes clear obituaries
tiffany drove too fast through a red light
because rafe, the bastard, hit her
for the thirtieth time, so she wanted to escape.
three others died in the accident, but
doubtless they were just as unhappy.

> albert collapsed, after eating a cake,
> from stress and depression, he turned
> to sugar and fats—oddly enough
> the president of the bakery died
> the same day from complications
> of fat-clogged arteries from overeating.

after learning he had heart disease, sam
followed the directions of those who
treated the symptoms of the problem;
he kept eating what he wanted and drinking

and overworking without enough sleep
until the treatment and his life killed them both.

      agnes simply lived to live, and she lived
      to be older than her friends. she never did much,
      never had an opinion, never gave to others,
      never risked her life, always let others,
      always let others work for her, always
      watch after her health. now, the number
      can finally be recorded: 100 years.

death practices by phone

hello, my name is death—what? death,
yes, no, i know your name. no, it's just
a survey. if you were to die this moment.
well, no, i was considering giving everyone
a brief advance notice, time for one last
statement—yes, a prayer, yes.
i'll come back later for—

okay, you're a lawyer; sure
you can make a plea but you won't be able
to afford the cost. Well, i don't know.
hell, i'd guess.

i understand you are a doctor
but in this situation, you're on earth
and it's nothing that death can't cure.
no, i don't think that it's absurd.

what do i believe, as death?
that you should make the place a little
better, not by trying, but just by living well,
consciously. and now i believe it is your time.

what? sorry mom, misdialed.
yes, okay, i'll wear them, yes, love you,

yes, said, love you! by the way,
how are you feeling?

who called me coyote?
i can find out where you are.
don't like that at all
you cannot hide forever.

no, not like that, think of it as the perfect
diet, the purity of bones unencumbered
by muscle or fat (which only the living
need), organs, skin, connective tissue—
well, you are no longer connected.

"death! how interesting!"
        "i know, i only personify dissolution,
but it works! you know, you understand how
lives are diced on time's noisy chopping board—
you know that echoes last longer
        than the brief cries of existence."
"so, death is silence?"
        "no, no, noise is existence
from the cries of pain to the popping and snapping
of quantum foam, unheard of course by beings
with ears."
            "death isn't funny!"
                            "why not?
the alternative is boring and serious."

death picks up
i am the angel of death.
    no it really makes no difference
    you will not be remembered
    even as a myth, for it is not you
    that's remembered anyway, just a pattern
    of what others think they saw. come now

i am the angel of death
　　what is your request?
　　you have only seconds left
　　be careful what you choose

"i am death, come for your body."
"what about my soul?"
　　　　"your soul died years ago."
"what! how i can i die without one, an immortal soul,
i thought ..."
　　　　"it is easy to die. just become nothingness,
　　　　　like the bubble after it pops."
"but, that's ridiculous how could my soul die first?"
　　　　　　　"it started with the first lie and accelerated
　　　　　　　with each false action and accusation,
　　　　　　　each wayward step, every insult ...
　　　　　　　you see?"
"but, my soul is immortal!"
　　　　　　"no, just a myth. each soul forms after
　　　　　　consciousness, flowering slowly but more
　　　　　　delicately than the brain or body,
　　　　　　than feeling or emotion. it is—"
"that's shit! i demand a hearing, a judge!"
　　　　　　"of course, i am patient, as patient as you.
　　　　　　i always listen—"
"no, someone else. your boss. god!"
　　　　　　"sorry, there is a partner, but we never
　　　　　　overrule one another. you have to make
　　　　　　the case with me ... or be silent."
"no, the soul is like a star, goethe said it shines
unceasingly"
　　　　　　"goethe was very smart, but look at the night
　　　　　　sky; what do you see?"
"stars, billions of stars."
　　　　　　"very good, but you cannot see
　　　　　　the trillions of invisible dead stars.
　　　　　　in deep time, even stars, like souls,
　　　　　　stop shining."
"oh."

"yes, you are facing death at last   put down that spray
    can, defacing death is not allowed, nice letter
    though, this cloth absorbs so much.
    now just release your hold ..."

death talks to himself
"no one understands. the tree of life is
the tree of death. you ascend
as you grow then you descend. the tree
is one giant exchange with the living
and non. the tree is, i am, all else is, or is not."

"death is not someone or something you know—
there is only a flow of holons in patterns
or the cultural, conscious, beating heart, the resting
corpse, the decaying statue, and finally
the forgotten words, all of which dissolve through
flowing time, as more are formed and replace
them and fade away themselves."

"yes, i know, it's old. i suppose i need a riding mower
now that the scythe has gotten rusty,
except for Africa—hmmmm, i'll have to keep it
and clean it for a while longer i guess. for europe a miata.
and for the pacific region a regatta ...
but what should i get for california? a hog,
a beamer, a volvo wagon?"

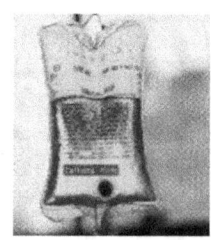

death takes a vacation

death parked his hummer in a handicapped space
near the entrance to dizneyworld; perhaps
he would help a few souls, then enjoy the rides
and confusion of people trying to be happy.
but, the first thing he saw on the way in was a coyote.
strange to see him not skulking in the bushes,
but strolling like any tired visitor or weary
canine family member. not just any coyote then,
but the mythic being who had stolen the sun.
he touched the radiation poisoning on coyote's tail
as he walked past, taking the last of that energy
and those crazy cells.
                    coyote flinched and looked up
but did not growl or run,
                    "i am sort of a trickster myself,"
said death.
            coyote snuffed, still disappointed by
his treatment in the cathedral of the mouse, but when
he felt a cold shiver and looked around, the hollow
man was gone. his tail did not itch.

on the way to the first ride, death saw someone to bless,
a blubbery guy named cam, whose overindulgence finally
was going to pay off: "i am death, i see you are in distress,
and you know there is nothing left."
                        "i, uh, did not expect
a person, just numbness and then darkness ... my heart?"
"yes, not enough exercise, the veins dried up. Here,
touch my hand."
            "okay, now what?"
                        "no argument, no last prayers?"
death was surprised.
            "no, i did this to myself.
i could have fasted, exercise and died later, but i chose
the path of pleasure. i could have shot ... where are we?"
"still here, just not visible to anyone."
                            "what am i now, then?"
"you are the echo of your consciousness, you will fade

into the vibrancy of all being, adding your echo
to the patterns of sound in trees and the flesh of weeds,
to all living flesh."
                    "then, there is nothing after life?"
"no, there is everything, but you must disperse completely
to participate in everything, you see, it is lighter now,
you can see fewer details, fewer edges, good bye now."
            "yes, yes."

after his next ride, the swirling teacups, death noticed
a woman watching him, a thin prim woman with a patrician
expression that he recognized from boston, or maybe
marblehead; her clothes had once been good. he walked to her.
        she introduced herself and asked if she was going to die.
he assured her that she would live a while longer.
        she said that she once was a doctor.
he replied that maybe she could have more than one purpose
in living.
        "what is it to die? she asked."
                            "you know, it is simply
to cease to breathe, for the heart to cease to beat, to cease
to live. it is the collapse of one level of complexity
to a simpler level. the you that is you disperses, leaving
only organs and cells that are no longer organized,
then they collapse and are prey to bacteria, viruses, sharks,
coyotes, all the things that break you down to pay
off your debt."
                "debt?"
"debt to nature, for all the lives that you took
so you could live, the lives you destroyed by accident,
or the ones you interfered with—"
                            "okay, okay, i got the idea.
somehow i thought you would be terse, a grim silent
reaper of souls."
                    "no, i always talk to people, especially the ones
who are afraid or the ones who want to know more."
        "what are you, exactly? the king of death?
the angel of death?"
                        "i prefer angel, but i am more like a spirit

outside of the normal dimensions of time."
                              "are you an angel like lucifer or gabriel?"
"no, i am not related to any one religion or belief. i am more
universal. i adhere to any being that is dying and observe
and participate in the process."
                              "i don't understand."
"and i can not explain it any better than i can explain
the reason for and expression of eleven dimensions in
my universe."
                              "don't you ever want to interfere in the process?"
"of course, and i do. some people are really not dying;
some can be helped with a kind word or touch. a few need
a push away so they do not ruin so many others lives."
                              "aren't you worried that you will alter the order
of the universe?"
                              "no, the order of the universe is what
we all make it, what we all contribute. without the ability
and power to choose, there would be much less reason
to live, don't you think?"
                              "yes, i am glad that you confirm my feelings
about choosing and changing things. thank you
for your time. are you here for a reason?"
    "of course, vacation, to rest and look around, but
i may do a little work while i am here. there is always
something that cannot wait, you know?"
                                          "yes, have fun."
"thank you," death replied, "and you also. feel
the breeze?"

after a few more silly rides, through darkness with large
scary figures or space themes, death went outside.
he stopped by a teen-aged boy in back of one of the stands,
saying: "i am the angel of death, i will wait until
you need me. do not worry, do not move."
    the boy's mouth moved but no sounds issued;
he was clearly frustrated that he could make nothing happen,
not sounds or movement.
    death cradled his head and watched the small bubbles
form at the corner of his mouth. when the confusion

left the boy's eyes, death showed him how
he would change, how it was good and how
it would benefit the cycle of life.

it was not a long day, although it was more interesting
than most. he reached into his pocket and took out a folder
that he found in the gift shop. it was for the holland america
line, for a cruise on the ship veendam. perhaps a cruise
would be relaxing. the people might be older
and more receptive to his messages. he smiled.
"i am death. come with me to shed this mortal coil
and to join the eternal flow that you call heaven. come
now, release your hold and enter the—"
what was he doing, practicing again?
he was on vacation.

death at work

applicant #4,300,3448.433
death: what?
      mr. 433: my soul, I said, what about my soul?
d: your soul is, i mean was, a delicate thing,
assembled by your sensitivity to others, and through
your attachment to a place. what was your place, exactly?"
      mr. 433: Umm, well, i don't know, miami, i guess.
d: miami? is that a real place now? i suppose. but, let's look
at your history here: detroit, portland, wilmington, buffalo,
la, chicago, miami. were you ever anchored somewhere?
probably not, you don't have a soul left. it was spread
so thin it evaporated with your travels. that happens.
      mr. 433: But, what will happen when i die?
d: nothing, i expect. nothing at all.

applicant #4,398,038,001
ms. 001: i know, i know. don't i get a second chance?
      death: no.
ms. 001: why not?

death: well, you had seconds, thirds, fourths.
you have had 74 years, two months, two weeks and three
days of life. that's over 27,000 days, over 650,000 hours,
300 million breathes, almost 3 billion heartbeats. wow!
did you think you had to go straight in line towards
　　　one goal? money?
ms. 001: not fair. i didn't just want money. i wanted happiness,
comfort, maybe a little fame.
　　　d: and were you alone in this universe?
ms. 001: of course not. i had a family. i—i want a second
chance. i deserve a chance to make things right
　　　d: they are right. or wrong. or it doesn't matter,
the balance is of the whole, not you. wait a minute, my cell
phone is vibrating. "hello, yes. yes, i was with 4,398,038,001.
sure, we were discussing her—
　　　oh for christ's sake. Yes i know, 'your' sake, then.
but, i don't like being called on particulars. maybe
we can trade. can i have falwell, now? he's at the end
of his usefulness. seriously, look at the man. how much lower
could he—oh, alright. okay. we'll talk soon."
　　　turning to the overweight real estate agent, death said:
"i'm not going to call it a second chance, let's call it a preview,
with the option to sell. get out of here. and be good."
　　　he looked at his running shoes and muttered,
　　　"damned do-gooder."

applicant #4,411,219,954
mrs. 954:"i'm on the toilet, go away!"
　　　death stood silently.
mrs. 954:"can i see some id please?"
　　　death showed her his fingertips.
mrs. 954:"someone will see me. i didn't agree to this!"
　　　d:"ah, yes, it's in the contract of life. death is part
of living, the last wonderful part in fact. where there is no
living there is no death—would you want to be a statue,
　　　lifeless and buried?"
mrs. 954:"yes, if it meant no decay!"
　　　d:"but you would not be living or aware—
　　　time carries its own annihilation."

mrs. 954:"come now, i have years to go, my doctor
has negotiated with the disease and i should live
another year."
   d:"the negotiations broke down, now come with me."
mrs. 954:"no, it is not my time. it is not right or fair!"
   d:"how can you argue?"
mrs. 954:"medicine has progressed, luxury has progressed
but not our ways of dying!"
   d:"no the ways of dying have progressed, the chemical
automotive, nuclear—"
mrs. 954:"no, i mean you, the way of death"
   d:"perhaps some things cannot be improved."
mrs. 954:"the horror is the time counting down, until only
years or seconds are left."
   d:"you have that backwards; time is being added
    to your life, until it extends—"
mrs. 954:"it's the aimlessness, the unknown uncertainty
i cannot stand. the fear of death, the fear of the words tagging
death, dying, departing, like some ugly taboo
that one cannot help but violate."
   d:"here is complete certainty, nothing to fear."

applicant #5,000,000,000
mr. 000:"take one the them, not me, the true one!"
   death:"the fundamental truth is that we all die,
    we have to die for renewal to happen."
mr. 000:"what is the goal of life? rightness, no, i meaning,
i mean—that is, no!"
   d:"a set of unique instants, never to be repeated,
   in the history of the universe, makes your life
   unique and meaningful.
mr. 000:"what do i get?"
   d:"the experience."
mr. 000:"nothing more?"
   d:"that is a true and precious treasure, now go."

deadlines

      "will you sleep with me?" sheila asked death,
who coughed and said "no, i never sleep."
      "no, you know, i mean have sex?"
  death sighed, thinking what was the attraction for some?
forbidden vapors? most were repelled and avoided looking
at death directly, "no, it would not be, ah, fitting."
      "literally?" she asked, touching his arm; she was interested
and had more questions: "are you the death of everything
living? how would you take an otter's soul?"
      "death becomes the image of death, and there are many other
images in other cultures and many other species. yes, i attend
other beings. for the beetle, i appear as a beetle,
the appropriate image, then i eat the head; for some trees
i am a fungus that links them to all other trees nearby.
a species of fly emerges from its larval state without a mouth,
and just enough energy to mate. the adult salmon digests
its own body before it mates, the last indigestible remainder
feeds others, the last regrets evaporate—
to them i appear as an explosion."

"what is the strangest death you witnessed?" the girl asked.
      death answered, "I think the death of equilibrium,
the new understanding that nature is a process pushed
by the pressure of life, continuously to greater and greater
heat and velocity."
      "must i die for some idea of balance?"
"what may be best for you may not help nature or the species.
the loss of an individual—" death paused and took a step
back as she touched his arm again, then continued, "how
can the loss of amphibians make a difference in warsaw?
how can a city change the temperature somewhere
and wipe out a line—death is not loss of harmony,
but part of larger—"
      "are you nervous?" she smiled, "are you the death
of water also? of air? of forests?"
      "unfortunately, yes, although these things are more
complex. to them i appear as a void—
and now we must disappear."

picnic at swan point
i was sitting by the stone angel, looking over
the small hills of stones carved with comforting
phrases: 'he's found eternal rest,' 'she rests in heaven now,'
'he's gone to a better place.'
one tombstone read: 'not dead, only sleeping,'
and no alarm will ever wake him either, i thought,
an oddly appropriate sentiment in a cemetery, which meant
in greek, to put to sleep. put to sleep by the kiss of death,
i laughed, not the phone call of death, or the handshake
of death, but then my phone rang and as i lifted it
to my lips i saw a cloud form over a gravestone
with a winged angel—winged death and through
the apparition i could read the carved words *momento mori*
(remember dying). the form reached out a hand,
which i ignored. "time for the diet of worms?" i spoke
into the phone.
        "if you wish," the form answered.
"no i prefer coyotes to worry the bones."
      "not your worry now," he whispered.

death, the final diet
"dead, the word is germanic in origin, is it not, meaning
mortal? does die come from diet?"
      "no," answered death, "diet is just a way of life."
"well, i'll finally be on a diet, now," art chuckled.
      "it isn't just about the purity of bones," death said
seriously. "you must have sinew and skin and even fat;
it is form."
      art faced his tormentor and said, "look, i'm just
overweight, certainly you can ignore me today? i've got
a meeting! i can't face death now!"
               but death ignored him
and continued: "facing death or defacing death
it doesn't matter as the face-off permits the skull to remain.
time to go—food is not a concern now, nor is that business
meeting. come."
      "wait, i need to have my body preserved."

"to keep it from the circuits of recycling?"
        "no, to be there for me at the end of time."
"it wouldn't be there, and it would interrupt the play of eater
and eaten, for surely we are eaten, if not by wolves,
then by worms. time to enter the play."

death has a crisis
"you are evil, god is the supreme good," the very
large woman said.
        death shrugged and answered: "no, even
god does not believe that, she knows she can not do
everything she wants or she would be as bad
a villain as you would make me."
    "i cannot die, my soul will live on."
"you are denying death. nice try. the soul is not a crop
harvested by perfect good," and death passed through her.

what does it mean to help people to die?
death asked himself. is that it? do they appreciate it? care?
do they want to know beforehand?
should he just shut up, take them, or continue to speak
with them, make them understand he cared that his touch
was the last they would feel and so much more
meaningful for that? no. what can he do then?
how could he leave his mark on the planet?
find meaning in his own existence?

"after the first, there is no other death," he said, the little
writer with the crooked bowtie.
        "no," said death himself, "every death is first
for the subject, and let us not lose sight of the individual
whose universe is scattering."
and death withdrew him.

death needed a special meaning, not as one of two
contrasting fictions: the romantic harvester or the brutal
destroyer of beauty and promise. no, he needed
a middle way.

125

death practices joking

is the reaper always grim? no. must he be ever serious?
no, he could joke, show people how to laugh
at death, make the reality less solemn but, first he needed
to practice, tell a few stories, relax the clients but, how?
what was funny about shuffling off the mortal coil?
banana peels? too crude too physical.
he could think up a good joke to tell so that laughter
would be the last sound and a smile the last
expression they knew. he considered: 'life is a terminal
disease' (he had seen the bumper sticker).
he could make up a joke: how many angels could fit
on the head of a pin? depended on the wingspan—
no that wasn't it. where did the idea for fountains
come from: vomiting.
why are peoples heads round: the ball inside rolls longer.
this was not going to work. he had to forget the jokes.
maybe for now he would just use their names
to appear more relaxed and friendly.
always leave 'em laughing? smiling? content?

death gets personal

death names amber

"amber, i'm here," death coolly intoned like a matinee
idol he remembered taking once.
                "i'm young, i know nothing of death,"
the young girl said,
        as death looked around her room at the posters
of the dead kennedys, comic book skeletal villains—
death images everywhere, but unreal beings sanitized
of real feelings; her parents had tried to spare her
any brush with death or unpleasantness from living
but that was pride, they should have taught her
the skill of mortality, the exchange of gifts,
the gifts of life and death.
he smiled and gave her a gift.

and willi

"did i fail to live to my ideal?" the hopi boy asked.
"did i have bad thoughts of the dead? are you an alus ghost?"
   "no, you are not two-hearted." death assured the boy.
"was it a witch? are you a witch?"
   "yes," death answered. "i am a repentant witch
and i must be a good shaman or i will die myself."
death knew this would please the boy
as they ghosted away.

kisho

"death is inevitable, the loss of everything dear
is unavoidable." kisho said.
                        and death relaxed.
"is this punishment for my mother?"
   "what do you think?" death asked, unrelaxing, knowing
the mother had threatened her death to admonish kisho
as a child, and he would believe as he would.
                 kisho bent slightly, "to the inevitable."

santosa

         "ah, the adjal," said santosa.
"yes, i have arrived, but it is not a predestined hour,
nothing is really predestined—"
                        "my death!"
"yes, but not the time," death said, looking around
the indonesian town, at the changes. "think of me as a 'talkin,'
the death whisperer of instructions."
         "what do i do?"
"nothing, no one really needs help, the process is easy.
there are no proper answers to the angel of death.
your soul has expressed its desires in dreams, so think
of this as a dream, but you will not want to wake."
         "ah, i am ready then."

bhudev

the helper woke in the morning and announced
that he was going to die, but would write a poem before
that event. then bhudev laid down his pen, called death
and i came.

       "i welcome you, death," bhudev said," i have
been prepared since i was thirteen. i am acquainted
with nonbeing. it is the same as before i was born. i wonder
if i helped many—"
       "tsk, tsk," i said, "the only answer
to some questions is: don't ask, especially if you know
the answer or that there is no answer."
       "i have chanted your name until i am living
         my life in shin-jin."
"well, you are right about not coming back, even as
a grasshopper," i said.
       "as long as it is right now." bhudev replied.

hjordis

"think of death as a teacher" death suggested.
       "yea, a dumb teacher, that tells not the student what
he needs to know." the scientist answered from his bed.
       "perhaps the lesson simply was not observed
by you before it applied to you," death offered,
"you never saw a songbird fall? your kitty cat get squished,
leaves, relatives lie still? notice the thread breaking?"
       "why wasn't i told?"
       "why would you have to be?
isn't it obvious? besides, being dumb means not speaking,"
       "no, i wasn't," hjordis noted, "everyone screamed
immortality, extension, new scientific fixes."
       "death is the only teacher at this level and here
no information passes to you, but that doesn't mean
it does not pass to the bacteria. your learning
should have been on the living side. here is lesson 'n.'"

kapera

"so you are an editor?" death noted, "I am kind of an editor
too, but i always say no, no more—or end!"

"but, you're not the creator."

"no, but creation would stop without my work. think
about it. if every yes were allowed to live, it would fill
existence with mediocrity— i eliminate all eventually
but certainly the unfit and dull immediately. imagine
steven king without an editor."

"bad example."

"oh, yes, right."

"immediately? i suspect not, have you looked
at our civilized gene pool lately? dullness triumphant."

"do you know what your name means?"

"yes, 'will die,' every name has a similar silent vowel."

"after you," death motioned politely.

lien

"your trouble," the candidate assessed his taker—
and death was the taker, not the maker—
"is that you areoneirotaxic."

"oh, please," death answered, "i never confuse
fantasy and reality. i know them both as one. you must
be onomatomanic, preoccupied with names and words,
and let it not be said that death is so easily undone.
now come."

"i want to be the one who escapes,
who continues as long as he likes," the librarian answered.

"but, why?" death asked, "you will never be ready,
no matter how long the extra time. now, exhale
and check out. the fine for overdue— ha, ha, ha, sorry
it just seemed so funny—"

"no, laughing becomes you, let's go then,
the split is made."

death meets his match

"epictetus said: 'death does not concern me.
when i am here, he is not'—"

      "A slight overlap, if you want—" death paused.

"i don't!" veren exclaimed, "maybe—"

and death nodded, the last of the day, before a rest.
veren continued: "have you ever eaten human flesh?"

"i don't eat," death said unnecessarily.

"i have. near the casuarina coast with the 'people.'
it was either that or become an edible."

      i hate taking anthropologists, death thought

"i know it is not about control, but its lack," veren said,
"although you can practice the art of dying, so popular
in spain at one time with the pestilence and war of
the 1400s. puppets were popular then, like this wolf puppet
here," and veren pointed to the top of his television set.
"what do you feel?" veren asked suddenly.

"understanding, respect," death answered.

"for me?" veren gawped, "certainly not."

"for the process, the matrix," death mused,
      remembering.

"is this a wild death or a tame one, mediated by love?"

"death is always wild," death said.

"how can you feel?" veren asked, "you're not real, like
a dream."

"you're are closer than you know. a dream is
the mind's way of integrating the day; and makes it meaningful;
in that way, i help you understand and summarize your life."

"so you're like a brain function?"

"i am independent of each brain, think of me as a spirit shared
by all living beings."

"like a god?"

"no, i have no powers, to save or change you."

"can you connect me with my wife?" veren asked.

"no, that connection died, but i can tell you she was not
worried about you, only michael."

"michael, yes, i understand, generations always take
the opposite road. is he—?"

      "i can tell you he is not

dead."

"thank you."

death asked, "what is your secret name?"

"i will not speak it," veren said, "it took too long
to find and tame it—it is the name of a dead man of course.
someday someone else will find mine and use it. thus
the dead live on in name. do you have such a name?"

"only what i call myself, and no, i will not tell."

"will you explain what is happening to me as it happens?"

"regrettably, i cannot. it is ineffable. do you have
any last words?"

"yes, even if there is no one to hear them:
the man is dead, long live the child."

about the author, reason, obviously a name used to protect
a reputation earned in a different field of activity
in the mainstream of the unstoppable machine—
anything else you need to know about her
can be found through her writings.

colophon

typeface: gillsans
display type: gillsans light
cover collage: a. m. caratheodory & nieman rian
graphics: a. m. caratheodory
design: riangarciacalusa